THE FORTUNES OF TEXAS

*Follow the lives and loves of a complex family
with a rich history and deep ties
in the Lone Star State.*

THE WEDDING GIFT

The town of Rambling Rose, Texas,
is brimming with excitement over the
upcoming wedding of five Fortune couples!
They're scheduled to tie the knot on
New Year's Eve, but one wedding gift
arrives early, setting off a mystery
that could send shock waves through the
entire Fortune family...

Despite her mother's disapproval,
Justine Maloney has no problem being
a single mom. So when her baby's father,
Stefan Mendoza, proposes a marriage of
convenience, she turns him down flat. If she
can't have all of Stefan, she'll take nothing at all.
Or that's what she tells herself.
But her heart has a mind of its own...

Dear Reader,

The wild and wonderful Fortunes are at it again!

Justine Maloney had a plan. Finish school. Get a job. Be independent. Maybe forget her mom's warnings about actions and consequences long enough to have a little fun along the way. A trip to Florida with her college BFFs should've been just the ticket. Miami's practically a universe away from her life in small-town Texas.

Only, the ticket came due nine months later.

What's a girl who is now the mom to the sweetest child in existence to do? Finish school. Do her job. Provide for the green-eyed baby boy who's the center of her world.

What could possibly happen?

Stefan Mendoza. That's what could happen. A man with his own plans—plans that have nothing to do with a particular Miami night he's never been able to forget. But when he walks into a small-town Texas coffee shop one June afternoon and sees his own eyes reflected in Justine's son's, all the plans in the world don't seem to matter a bit.

What's a woman to do? What's a man to do?

Probably make a few more mistakes. Probably figure out how to get past them. And hopefully learn that doing it all *together* is the sweetest plan of all.

Hope you enjoy their lesson!

Allison

Finding
Fortune's Secret

—

ALLISON LEIGH

HARLEQUIN

SPECIAL
EDITION

Special thanks and acknowledgment are given to
Allison Leigh for her contribution to
The Fortunes of Texas: The Wedding Gift miniseries.

HARLEQUIN®
SPECIAL
EDITION™

Recycling programs
for this product may
not exist in your area.

ISBN-13: 978-1-335-40857-0

Finding Fortune's Secret

Copyright © 2022 by Harlequin Enterprises ULC

For questions and comments about the quality of this book,
please contact us at CustomerService@Harlequin.com.

Harlequin Enterprises ULC
22 Adelaide St. West, 41st Floor
Toronto, Ontario M5H 4E3, Canada
www.Harlequin.com

Printed in U.S.A.

Though her name is frequently on bestseller lists, **Allison Leigh**'s high point as a writer is hearing from readers that they laughed, cried or lost sleep while reading her books. She credits her family with great patience for the time she's parked at her computer, and for blessing her with the kind of love she wants her readers to share with the characters living in the pages of her books. Contact her at allisonleigh.com.

Books by Allison Leigh

Harlequin Special Edition

Return to the Double C

A Weaver Christmas Gift
One Night in Weaver...
The BFF Bride
A Child Under His Tree
Yuletide Baby Bargain
Show Me a Hero
The Rancher's Christmas Promise
A Promise to Keep
Lawfully Unwed
Something About the Season
The Horse Trainer's Secret
A Rancher's Touch
Her Wyoming Valentine Wish

The Fortunes of Texas: Rambling Rose

The Texan's Baby Bombshell

The Fortunes of Texas: The Hotel Fortune

Cowboy in Disguise

Visit the Author Profile page
at Harlequin.com for more titles.

*This book is dedicated to my daughters,
who impress me every day.*

Prologue

Seventeen months ago,
Miami, Florida

Thank goodness for sunglasses.

Justine Maloney adjusted hers as she left the shady interior for brilliant sunlight. Despite the dark lenses, she still winced. Sunshine compounded by an enormous, glittering pool.

Not helpful to a hangover.

It was New Year's Day. Miami was twenty degrees warmer than it was back in Texas. The luxurious hotel was a dream and the only thing she'd needed to pay for was her flight to get there.

Yes, she'd had to raid her savings to afford that

plane fare, but that was a drop in the bucket compared to what the long holiday weekend had to be costing.

Staying buried in her huge bed in the over-the-top suite bemoaning her actions the night before would have been ungrateful. Nearly criminal.

So here she was. Teeth brushed. Cutoff shorts. Tankini top. Wishing that her sunglasses could do a better job of protecting the throbbing inside her head.

She scanned the people sprawled on the lounges surrounding the pool, finally spotting Garland and Debbie. There was no sign of Anika though, and she was the whole reason they were there in Florida at all.

Anika was soon to marry a Miami businessman who could afford hotel suites like theirs. She'd never have to worry again about saving her precious dimes.

Instead, Anika's fiancé, Victor, was treating them to one last hurrah before he swept Anika off for their wedding on a private island in the Bahamas.

Every step Justine took sent pain ricocheting inside her skull. By the time she dumped her book bag on the empty lounge chair next to her friends, she'd promised life and the universe that she would never drink again.

Debbie squinted over the top of her own sunglasses. "Damn, Jus."

"Surprised you're upright," Garland added. Along with her sunglasses, she wore a wide-brimmed hat that was a lot more about fashion than function.

"Since you spent half the night on the bathroom floor."

"Happy New Year to you, too." Justine gingerly sat next to her book bag. "Nice how you make a girl feel good about herself."

Debbie snickered. "Last I saw of you at the party, you were dancing with Tall, Dark and Do Him. From the looks of you, I'm guessing there was no *do*."

Mortification burned inside her.

Pretty hard to seduce someone when you were puking into a bush while your intended quarry held back your hair.

It was a wonder she hadn't been kicked out of the hotel.

Garland rolled onto her stomach. "Still poor virginal Justine."

This was the problem with getting together with her old dorm-mates. They knew all her secrets.

"It's only when I'm around all of you that I even think about that," she complained. "I should've lied. Told you I'd met someone and done the deed. None of you would've known differently." She was twenty-three years old. She couldn't possibly be the last virgin on earth, even if it sometimes felt that way.

"You could've *tried* lying," Debbie said with a snort. "Except you're the worst liar on the planet. Always have been."

Garland's laugh sounded muffled against her folded arms. "Unlike Anika. Can you believe she convinced Victor that she graduated top of our class?"

Much better to think about their missing fourth than to think about Stefan of the night before. Rather than run for the nearest exit when Justine tore out of his arms to race for the nearest bush, he'd been solicitous personified. Which made it even more embarrassing. Every other guy on the planet would have left her slinking back to her room in anonymous shame.

Stefan hadn't been satisfied until he'd escorted her right to her hotel room door.

Actions have consequences, Justine. How often have I told you that?

Add her mother's voice to the misery that was her throbbing head.

She squinted at the palm trees surrounding the infinity-edge pool. "Where is Anika, anyway?"

"Lunching on caviar and champagne in the presidential suite with Victor, no doubt." Debbie's tone was acidic. "Even though this trip was supposed to be about the four of *us*."

"She met us all at the airport," Justine reminded. They'd all come in at different times from varied locations. "Until Victor showed up last night at the party, it's been like old times."

Garland laughed and raised an arm, rubbing her fingers against her thumb. "But with *dinero*."

"Yeah, well, money isn't everything, is it? I'm not one for caviar but I *am* getting hungry. I'm ordering something from the pool bar." Debbie pushed off her lounge and walked away, her caftan fluttering behind her.

Justine chewed the inside of her cheek. "She's not really mad at Anika, is she?"

"Nah." Garland flicked open the back of her bikini top. "It just annoys her that she and Todd won't get down the aisle before Anika does."

"At least when Deb and Todd get married we won't have to worry about not making the cut for a destination wedding," Justine said without heat. The private island that Victor had rented out could only accommodate two-dozen people. With his and Anika's large families, the guests had been kept strictly to their immediate relations.

Thus his gift to Anika of bringing in her girlfriends for the holiday weekend instead.

"Deb and Todd'll get married in their Minnesota barn and we'll be escorted by cows," Garland predicted with a visible shudder. She'd been raised in Dallas and was a city girl, through and through. Now, she worked in Chicago with a corporate events planner and lived in an apartment she claimed was even smaller than the Houston dorm room the four of them had once shared. She reached out and pushed her knuckles against Justine's shin. "Sorry it didn't work out with Stefan. You looked like you were really interested in him."

Justine lifted her shoulder, which set off another wave of throbbing inside her skull. "I had my chance with a gorgeous guy and I blew it. I'll survive." She moved her squashy hat over her face, hoping to end the topic.

Garland ignored the hint. "Don't be so defeatist."

She pulled aside the hat again. "Stefan wouldn't have given me the time of day if it hadn't been for you and Deb." Between the dress that Garland loaned her and the makeup and hair that Deb had helped with, Justine hadn't looked anything like herself when the four of them had walked into the lavish party the previous evening. Add a lot of wine and a lot of nudging from her friends, and somewhere she'd found the nerve to ask Stefan to dance when he'd shown up with Victor.

When Stefan had guided her out to the poolside palm grove to dance beneath the stars, she'd been giddy. He was tall. Handsome. He danced like a dream and in his arms, dusty little Chatelaine, Texas, had felt a million miles away. She wasn't studious, virginal Justine who lived with her mama because she couldn't afford anything else.

She was Cinderella and he was the totally hot prince.

It was only now in the cold light of hangover and sunshine that she realized he'd treated her more like an indulgent uncle than a prospective lover.

Not that she had an uncle.

But she could imagine.

"It wasn't the dress *or* the makeup. You've never given yourself enough credit," Garland said.

Justine gave Garland the stink eye. "You're the siren. Anika's the ingenue, and Debbie's the earth mother. What was my role? Giving guys advice on how to get the attention of one of *you* three, that's what."

Garland laughed heartily and Justine pinched the pain inside her forehead. "How is it that you're not suffering? Anika's the only one who didn't drink."

"Clean living," Garland said facetiously. Holding her bikini in place, she flipped over again, and her long hair streamed over the side of the chaise.

"Here." Debbie returned with a tall bottle of water that probably cost as much as the used textbook in Justine's bag. "Hydrate."

Justine took the bottle and twisted off the fancy silver cap. "Thanks." She guzzled down a third of it, and the fact that it didn't want to come right back up was a good sign.

When the waiter arrived with a platter of fish tacos, though, she shuddered and closed her eyes.

By the time Anika appeared a few hours later and snuggled onto the lounge next to Justine, she felt somewhat better.

"You and Stefan looked *really* cozy last night," Anika said. Her eyes danced. "So, did you do the deed?"

Justine groaned and slouched further down the chaise lounge. "Don't ask."

"She'll forever be the unforgettable woman to him," Garland said with a laugh.

Justine grimaced. "Very funny."

"Oh." Anika pouted slightly. "I thought the two of you looked meant to be."

"Like you and Victor, I suppose," Debbie said dryly.

"We are meant to be." Anika smiled beatifically. "I can't wait to be his wife. To have his babies."

Garland made a choking sound. "What decade is this? What about a career?"

Anika waved a dismissive hand. "Victor's not getting any younger and having babies is the only thing I've ever really wanted to do. Life's short. We've got to love hard." She bumped her shoulder against Justine's. "What about you? Don't you want kids?"

"Eventually, maybe. But only after I finish my graduate degree. After I'm fully established in my career. That's when I'll start thinking about relationships and family."

Anika's smile widened. "You'll meet the right guy, just like I met Victor, and suddenly your plans will feel a lot less important."

Justine laughed at that. "Only *you* would end up with a man like Victor, sweetie. The stars just align themselves for you. Me? I'm the one who loses her lunch when Mr. Perfect comes around."

"Mr. Perfect, huh?" a deep voice said behind her.

Butterflies filled her stomach and no amount of regret for the night before could overcome a thrilling stab as she looked over her shoulder.

The night before, Stefan's boldly patterned black-

and-white shirt had kept his suit from looking too formal. Today, he was all sorts of casual. Collarless, untucked shirt. Linen pants that were just the right amount of slouchy.

His olive-toned skin was tanned; his thick hair was as dark as obsidian, and his distinctively mossy green eyes were just as magnetic as she'd remembered.

And he wasn't looking at her as if she'd totally blown her chances at all...

Chapter One

"I hear you have the best café Cubano in all of Texas," Stefan Mendoza said when the young woman inside Kirby's Perks greeted him.

Her name tag said Bonita, and her smile was dimpled. "I don't know about *all* of Texas," she allowed, "but here in Rambling Rose?" She toyed with the long string of the apron tied around her trim waist. "How about if I serve it up and if it doesn't make the grade, you keep coming back for a week until I get it right. On the house."

Stefan grinned. Flirting—giving and receiving—was as natural to him as breathing. It was to most of the Mendozas.

He leaned his elbow on the counter as if he had

all the time in the world, though he didn't. "Not sure that's the best way to make a profit, Bonita."

"Guess that ought to prove how confident I am that you'll be pleased."

Subtext received. "One *cafecito*, then. Thank you."

"It'll be a few minutes," she warned. "We grind our own coffee beans."

"Anything worthwhile is worth waiting for."

"A man with patience. I like that. What's your name?"

"Stefan."

"All right, Stefan. Hold on to your hat." She began measuring beans into a grinder.

He glanced at his watch. Just after three o'clock. The perfect time for the Cuban version of espresso whether his brother was waiting for him over at Provisions or not.

The restaurant that Mark's wife owned with her sisters served many excellent things. But their Cuban coffee missed the mark—at least in his opinion. Same went for the sisters' other restaurant, Roja.

All told, Stefan had been in Texas two years. But ever since leaving Miami, he'd been on an unending hunt for the perfect café Cubano.

He idly drummed his fingers on the counter and glanced around the coffee shop. There weren't any other customers at the moment, but Stefan knew the place was popular. The smell of coffee was redolent. The decor welcoming enough—there was even a

kid-sized table and chairs situated in one corner—
but when he thought coffee, he still envisioned
the vibrant color and chaos at his favorite place in
Miami's Little Havana district. The last time he'd
been to Morgan's was more than a year ago. It was
the last time he'd had a truly perfect *cafecito*.

Last time he'd had a truly perfect night with a
woman, too.

Which meant that now, he couldn't think about a
cafecito without thinking about *her*.

Justine hadn't been related to the business he'd
been conducting in Miami. But the few brief hours
that they *had* shared?

He'd been measuring every female since against
them.

Another customer came in and Stefan wandered
over to study a display of travel mugs. When the
newcomer started in on a laundry list of an order
to Bonita, he sent a text message to his brother that
he was running a few minutes late. It was obvious
the customer was taking the large order back to her
beauty salon to share.

It dawned on him that he should probably have
done the same thing. Ordered a *colada* which he
could share with Mark and Megan instead of a one-
shot *cafecito* for only himself. Regardless of the
name, the liquid gold in the cup was the same. And
it would be a nice gesture. A reminder of days past
when he and his brothers had all still lived in their
native Miami. The first time Stefan had ever stepped

foot inside Morgan's had been with Mark. He'd been ten. Mark, six years older, had driven them there.

Bonita was making change for the other customer while keeping an eye on the worn-looking pot sitting on an electric burner that she'd plugged in next to the commercial-style espresso machine. He took it as a good sign she was going old-school with the *moka* pot. "Bonita, is it too late to change that to the whole *colada*?"

The other customer was visibly startled. "Kirby's has cocktails now?"

Bonita laughed. "Not a piña colada with rum, Lindy. Stefan's talking about Cuban coffee."

Lindy made a face. "Bummer. Imagine the crew at Live and Let Dye if I came back with cocktails and cookies?"

Bonita laughed again and flipped open the top of the *moka* pot to watch for the first drips of coffee to emerge and began selecting cookies from the pastry case. She'd just finished boxing them when she yanked the pot off the burner and poured a few thick, syrupy drops over the sugar she'd already spooned into the bottom of a small silver pitcher. She stuck the pot back on the burner to finish percolating, punched a few buttons on the espresso machine to continue filling Lindy's order and began mixing the sugar concoction vigorously with a spoon.

Stefan's mouth was already watering.

"You look very familiar to me." Lindy was giving him a look beneath artificially long lashes. "Ever been to the Live and Let Dye salon?"

He shook his head. "Nope. Sorry."

"I'm just sure we've met. What's your name again?"

"Stefan Mendoza."

"Ah." She nodded. "I bet you're related to Mark and Rodrigo."

"Brothers."

"I'm telling you, I have a talent." She tapped the edge of her credit card against the counter while Bonita continued whipping the sugar into a deep gold, caramel-colored paste. "I'm Lindy, by the way. When you need someone to run her fingers through your hair—"

"Give it a rest, Lindy." Bonita finished her frenzied stirring and began pouring the rest of the espresso into the sugar mixture. "He's a customer."

Lindy grinned, giving him as bold a look as Bonita had done earlier. "He's not my customer. Yet." She winked. "Come visit me over at the salon when it's time for a cut, sugar. We're just around the block. First style's on the house."

Stefan chuckled. "Have to say, in the month I've been here, Rambling Rose is turning out to be a welcoming place."

"We like to think so." Bonita poured Stefan's coffee into a full-sized foam cup and set it on the counter along with several shot-sized plastic cups stacked together.

Lindy snorted. "You've lived here all of a month, too, Bonita." She propped her hand on her shapely hip and looked at Stefan again. "Whereas *I* have been here all my life."

Stefan was barely paying attention. The creamy sugar foam had risen to the top of the strong coffee and because he wasn't always the most patient of men, he filled one of the small cups halfway. Just enough to have a taste. The coffee smelled almost exactly right. He swirled it slightly, watching the *espuma* sitting on the surface cling and slide against the plastic walls of the little cup.

"You look like you're sampling wine," Lindy said.

He grinned. "I do plenty of that, too." He drank the tiny sample of coffee. It was blistering hot.

Not nirvana. But close.

Bonita was watching him, smiling expectantly.

He set down the empty cup and pulled out his wallet.

Ironic as hell that he'd come to a small town located halfway between Austin and Houston to pay five times what he would have paid for the same coffee back in Florida, but beggars couldn't be choosers. "Worth the wait," he said, handing over the cash.

"Does that mean you'll be back?" Her fingers brushed his deliberately.

He was mildly intrigued with her. Emphasis on the mild. His hunt for the perfect Cuban coffee was as fruitless as meeting a woman who could compete with a memory. "Count on it." He stacked the small cups on top of the larger one and smiled at both women. "Ladies."

He left the coffee shop and climbed in his truck—another thing that he'd changed since moving to Texas. He'd never thought he'd want to drive anything but a sports car. At least with the truck he didn't have to fold himself into a pretzel to climb behind the wheel *and* he was able to haul cases of Mendoza wine around when he needed to. It'd be equally useful when it came to Rising Fortune beer.

He glanced at his watch again. Ten minutes late for his meeting with Mark.

Hopefully, walking in with the *colada* would make up for it.

Making up for resigning from Mendoza Winery? That could be a tougher nut.

Mark's brows rose when Stefan set the cups on the table where he was sitting with an opened laptop near the bar inside Provisions.

"Sorry I'm late." He filled two smaller cups with the hot brew.

Mark picked up the shot-sized cup and swirled it the same way that Stefan had. "Told you Kirby's Perks had a good one." He squinted slightly as he took a drink and sighed deeply. "Damn. That's the best one yet. Kirby make it?"

"Someone named Bonita." Stefan pulled out the chair across from his brother. "Sounded like she's new there."

Mark took another sip. "Reminds me of Morgan's and the old days."

"What old days?" Megan appeared next to their table. She was the financial officer for the restaurants that she owned with her fellow triplets Ashley and Nicole. Since Mark had married Megan last New Year's and Rodrigo had married Ashley the year before that, and Nicole was executive chef at Roja—which he'd frequented almost daily while he'd been staying at Hotel Fortune waiting for his house deal to close—he was finally able to see the subtle differences between them.

"Miami days." Mark tugged her down beside him and poured her a little cup. "Stefan brought it from Kirby's Perks."

Megan and her sisters hailed originally from Florida, too, but instead of partaking the near bliss-in-a-cup, she waved her hand. "I don't need my heart jumping out of my chest from a caffeine bullet like that."

Stefan considered suggesting she give it to Tom who was working behind the bar, as an example of a proper café Cubano, but he kept it to himself. If neither Rodrigo nor Mark had offered constructive criticism over the matter with their wives—who actually owned the place—then he had no business doing so.

Even before they'd founded the winery that bore their name, the Mendozas had always been involved in restaurants. In nightclubs. Aside from his initial investment to buy the winery in the first place, Stefan's particular expertise was marketing and he was successful enough in that regard, though Mark was a whiz at marketing himself.

Pretty much whatever Stefan thought up when it came to marketing their wines, Mark had already done it sooner, and often better. Rodrigo, only two years older than Stefan, had ended up making his own place in the world by founding Vines Consulting Group when the family business had gotten too confining. And then he'd also become partners in the development of Hotel Fortune.

Stefan was thirty years old. He'd made money with the winery. They all had. But he needed a new challenge. His own challenge. Outside of the Mendoza wine world.

"Okay," Mark tapped his empty cup on the table, "what was the big thing you wanted to talk about today?"

Figure on Mark to be practically reading Stefan's mind. He opened his mouth to speak but a squeal of delight stopped him.

"Is that what I think it is?" Ashley pounced on the little cup as if she'd found a loose diamond.

"Have at it," Megan said with a laugh and her sister wasted no time in taking a sip.

Ashley gave a quick, shivering sigh and twirled on her high heel. "Don't tell me there's a new coffee shop in town."

"Kirby's," Stefan said. "New barista."

"What has my wife dancing in the middle of the afternoon?"

She sauntered over to Rodrigo who was walking in from the back-office area and hung her arm around his neck. "Just a little *cafecito* delight."

He took the small cup from her and finished it off. "Not bad." He looked at them over his wife's head. "Remember Morgan's in Little Havana?"

Stefan smiled wryly.

"Mark was the first one to take me there," Rodrigo reminisced.

"Dad took Carlo and Chaz and me when we were still kids," Mark said, citing their other brothers.

"Speaking of Dad," Rodrigo said as he steered Ashley toward their table, "did you hear he took Mrs. Shevchenko with him to Costa Rica? Stef, you dated Missy Shevchenko when you were in high school, didn't you?"

Stefan nodded. "I talk to Dad all the time." Whether Esteban was in Austin or in Miami where he still had a house, Stefan talked to him routinely. "He hasn't mentioned he's dating her mom." Much less that he'd taken a companion on his trip.

"Maybe not to you," Rodrigo said. "But sounds to me like it's getting serious."

"Dad, serious?" Mark shook his head immediately. "Never."

"Besides," Ashley said as she perched on the chair next to Stefan, her expression mischievous, "you Mendoza boys always fall for Fortune girls."

For some reason they all looked at Stefan. "What're you looking at me for? I'm not the one who's put my head in that particular noose."

"Noose?" Ashley punched his arm none too gently.

Rodrigo gave Stefan a *when did you get stupid?* look. "Gotta admit, all of us *have* married Fortunes."

"Well, I'm not," Stefan said flatly. "No disrespect to those here of that particular persuasion," he added before Ashley could slug him again. "I'm not marrying anyone else either." The topic made his collar feel tight. "Dad and I will be the last single Mendozas. Regardless of what he's doing with Terry Shevchenko. Though," he smiled reminiscently, "if she's anything like Missy, they're probably havin' a helluva time."

"That's right." Mark's gaze sharpened with remembrance. "She was your first—" He broke off and gave Megan a quick look as if she'd just kicked him beneath the table.

The others laughed.

"All right, well, as entertaining as this is," Megan said as she kissed Mark's cheek before standing, "I have work to do. So, I'll leave you boys to it."

"And I have things to do as well," Ashley said. She handled everything front-of-house for Provisions and even though she and her sisters had been incredibly young when they opened the place, they'd proven their success over the last few years. She stroked Rodrigo's cheek and sashayed away.

Rodrigo finally dragged his gaze from his wife's rear view and sat next to Mark. He drained the last mouthful of coffee still left in the foam cup. "When was the last time you went to Morgan's?"

Mark squinted, thinking. "Four, five years at least."

"A year and a half or so," Stefan answered when Rodrigo looked at him. He could have told him how many weeks. How many days. Probably even how many hours, but that would make it seem like he'd been mooning over Justine.

Mark looked at his watch. "I've got a conference call in about five. What was it you wanted to talk about?"

Stefan stifled his frustration. He'd planned to float the news to Mark first before breaking it to everyone else. But it was Stefan's fault for being late in the first place and Rodrigo didn't look like he was going anywhere any time soon.

"I'd hoped for a little more time to get into this, but since that's a bust I'll just get to it." He took a breath, irritated with himself that it suddenly felt hard to get out the words. "I'm resigning from Mendoza Winery."

Silence ensued.

Mark's eyes narrowed.

Rodrigo's eyebrows lifted.

They might have heard crickets chirping if not for Ashley talking on the phone on the other side of the restaurant.

Stefan leaned back and hung his arm over the empty chair next to him. He looked out the windows. Whistled a soundless tune.

Mark finally closed his laptop and sat forward. "Did the deal fall through on that old house?"

That old house sat on nine acres of land. Land that figured prominently in Stefan's plans. "Kind of hard for that to happen when escrow closed two weeks ago, and I've moved in." Yeah, he was living out of boxes and would be for some time while renovations dragged the place into the current century, but that was beside the point.

"Then I don't get it," Mark said. "What's gone wrong?"

"*Nothing's* gone wrong."

Mark wasn't listening. "Everyone made a fortune when you landed the distribution deal with Victor Montenegro. It's too bad it ended the way it did after his death last year. But I warned you not to sink all your savings into buying that old ranch. Never put all your eggs in one basket. Remember?"

"This isn't about the Montenegro deal. Or me buying the ranch outright. I still have savings—strange as that might seem to you—and *this* is a perfect example of why I'm backing away from the winery."

"*What's* an example?"

"No matter what I accomplish, I'm always the kid brother!"

"Dude. You *are* the youngest," Mark pointed out as if it was news.

"Don't be a jackass." Stefan gestured at Rodrigo. "He knows what I mean."

Rodrigo looked resigned. "You want a fresh challenge." He glanced at Mark. "And he doesn't mean real estate or working with you on opening a new channel for the winery."

"Montenegro Hospitality Group. Cooper Promotions." Mark ticked off his fingers. "Product placement in that streaming series last year and the Grayson Gear commercials this year. You're the one who brought in those deals. Major, profitable deals. And you want us to *buy* you out of your share?"

Stefan muttered an oath. "I'm not talking about pulling out my investment! I'm just talking about the day-to-day work." He shoved at his irritation. "Look," he said more calmly. "Mendoza Wine is great. It'll be great whether I'm part of the payroll or not. And since we first got it off the ground…you know. The challenge is waning."

Mark silenced the beep from his watch. "Why didn't you just say something earlier? What's the plan? And don't tell me ranching. Playing polo since you were fifteen doesn't qualify you for—"

"I bought nine acres," Stefan cut him off. "Not a damn ranch running cattle. And I'm going into business with Adam Fortune. He's brewing the best craft beer around, and by the time I'm finished, the rest of the country is going to think so, too."

"We're already serving Rising Fortune's IPA at Provisions," Rodrigo said. "When we can get it."

"Exactly. When you can get it. Which is why Adam needs to expand out of his small set up. I got Mendoza Wines into the places I have, and I can do the same with Rising Fortune. Once we've conquered Texas and if our production levels can support it, we'll work on the southwestern states and see where it goes from there."

"Yeah, but marketing is marketing," Mark said. "You're just exchanging wine for beer. One job for another."

"No, I'm going into *partnership* with Adam. A full partnership. Adam and his wife own the seven-acre plot next to mine. We've got the licensing and the zoning nearly taken care of and we plan to build the new brewery on our common border. He's already outgrown his current setup and it's not even two years yet. He's got the brewing expertise. But I've got the marketing. We signed the partnership agreement a month ago. When we founded Mendoza Winery, it was because we bought out Hummingbird Ridge. But Adam and I are building Rising Fortune from the ground up."

Mark looked at Rodrigo. "The two of you are usually thick as thieves against the rest of us. You didn't know anything about this either?"

"I knew he's been talking with Adam for a while." Rodrigo gave Stefan an inscrutable look. "I didn't know it had progressed as far as it did."

Stefan wasn't going to feel bad for not cluing him in first. "Rodrigo, you've made a business out of telling people how to improve every aspect of what they're doing. Win, lose or draw, I *need* to do this myself." Of all his brothers, Rodrigo should understand that.

"Stubborn," Mark said. "You've always been stubborn."

Stefan shrugged. "Runs in the family." He sat forward. "I don't intend leaving you in a lurch. It's going to take time for Rising Fortune Brewing to hit its stride. I'll still manage all my current accounts until you can figure out someone else to take over. But when it comes to creating new business, it's only fair that you know where my focus is going to be."

"Do you expect me to tell the others?" Mark asked. "What about Alejandro?"

Stefan shook his head, annoyed again. "No. But you're the one I work most closely with for the day-to-day, so I figured you should be the first. I plan to talk to Alejandro next." Their cousin still acted as the company's CEO.

Mark spread his hands. "I don't know whether to pound you on the back in congratulations or thump you on the head for creating a new headache for me."

"You could *try* thumping me." Stefan didn't bother hiding his grin as he pushed away from the table and stood. The worst was over. He knew his brothers. Whether they thought he was defecting or not, they'd still have his back. Same as he had theirs. "But we both know I'd kick your ass."

"Please." Mark snorted as he opened his laptop

once again. "I'm going to hold you to taking care of your current accounts," he warned, but he had a faint smile on his face. "Now go on so at least *I* can get back to work."

Rodrigo gave Stefan a clap on his back as they walked out to the parking lot. "I could look over your business plan," he offered. "I'd even give you the friends and family discount."

With the utmost respect and brotherly love, Stefan gave him a one-fingered salute and got in his truck.

Rodrigo was still laughing in the rearview mirror as Stefan drove away.

Euphoria fueled Stefan even more than caffeine. When he drove past Kirby's Perks again on his way out to his new home, he wheeled around and parked on the street in front.

There was nothing wrong with mild interest.

Bonita was pretty. She could make a decent Cubano. He could do worse.

Whistling under his breath, he got out and headed through the glass door.

Two people stood in line at the counter. He spotted Bonita working alongside a much older woman. Bonita offered him a knowing smile. "Back for another already?"

He smiled, too. "Back for something."

Her smile widened. "Be with you in a few."

Certain they were on the same wavelength, he glanced around at the tables, prepared to wait.

A pale girl with heavy dark hair and bracelets

stacked halfway up her arms stared dreamily out the window. At another table, a middle-aged redhead was giving the laptop in front of her more attention than the stroller beside her. On top of the empty table between them, a stack of thick books sat to one side of an oversize latte cup.

He looked to the other side of the room. There was an unoccupied easy chair next to the kids' corner where a little boy with blond hair was stacking blocks. The middle-aged woman ordering at the counter kept looking over, giving him the side-eye as if he was getting too close to the boy.

He bypassed the chair and leaned against the wall next to the closed restroom door instead and crossed his arms.

He'd take Bonita to Roja, he decided and pulled out his phone, debating whether he'd need a reservation. He was in the mood to celebrate. And not in the mood to have to wait in line. Hotel Fortune wasn't the kind of place that rented by the hour, but if it so happened that things progressed to a shared night…?

He dialed the restaurant at the hotel and held the phone to his ear. Next to him, the restroom door opened and he turned away slightly, listening to the ringing.

"It's a great afternoon at Roja," a cheerful voice replaced the ringing. "This is Mariana. How can I help you today?"

He leaned against the wall again. Mariana Sanchez was one of his favorite people at Roja. She had a big bun of blond hair and an even bigger personality. "Hey there, Mariana. You're usually in the kitchen. What're you doing answering the phone? This is Stefan Mendoza—"

Ceramic shattered and his attention jerked toward the noise the same way everyone else's did. The only thing that didn't go momentarily silent was the nonsensical babble that he realized was coming from inside the baby stroller.

Coffee cup down. Coffee spilled everywhere.

"Well, hey there, handsome!" Mariana's voice sounded loud through the phone. "Little early for your usual take-out order, isn't it?"

"I wanted to get a reservation." His gaze trailed past the broken cup shards to the sandaled feet standing in the middle of them.

Slim ankles. Sleek calves.

"Sure thing, sweetie pie," Mariana chirped in his ear.

Tanned thighs. Denim shorts. Skin barely peeking below the hem of a gauzy white blouse with blue stitching.

Memory whispered inside him.

His gaze kept going.

"What time you thinking, Stefan?"

He wasn't even aware of sliding his phone into his pocket or the unconscious step he took toward her.

Honey-blond hair.

Eyes distinctively caramel brown.

The same color as the *espuma* on Morgan's café
Cubano.

Seventeen months, he thought.

Five hundred and fourteen days.

Countless hours. Endless minutes.

"Justine?"

Chapter Two

Justine felt the blood draining out of her head as she watched him—Stefan Mendoza—head her way.

She was dizzy. Rooted in place. Lukewarm latte dripped down her shin. Her big toe stung where the cup had shattered.

"Justine!" His voice was deep. His green gaze searching hers. "It's really you."

Not just dizzy. Almost sick to her stomach.

The amount of time she'd spent dreaming about him far exceeded the amount of time they'd actually spent together. That hadn't even been two days. Hours, really.

With one exception, they were the most memorable hours of her entire life.

"Your hair's shorter." He stopped only when Hillary rushed between them with a rag in hand.

Feeling oddly separated from the action, she saw her hand lift. Felt her hair between her fingertips when she touched it. Lindy over at Live and Let Dye kept it cut for her at shoulder length now. Ever since—

She looked at the stroller next to her table. It was an oversize thing. Expensively made. Like nothing *she* could ever afford—more like an upholstered bassinet on wheels with a big sun canopy over the top of it.

She dropped her hand and collapsed, ungainly, back onto her chair.

"I like it." Stefan had a faint smile on his face. As if he couldn't believe his eyes.

"Thank you," she mouthed politely. Soundlessly.

"Oh, hon," Hillary tsked. "You're bleeding." She'd begun wiping up the mess, gathering the broken bits of the ceramic mug in her towel. "I'll get some clean towels and a fresh latte." She sidled around Stefan who'd neared enough to touch Justine's stack of textbooks.

"Still studying, I see."

Justine was aware of Kirby's Perks' other regulars watching them. Rebecca and Annette. She considered them friends. But right now, the two of them—along with everyone else—were looking at her.

Judging her?

Finding her just as wanting as her own mother did?

Stefan was still staring as if he couldn't quite believe what he was seeing.

She realized she still hadn't answered his question about what she was studying. "Social work," she managed.

"Can't tell you how often I've thought about you."

Her foolish, foolish heart picked up its silly head.

"After Victor's plane—" He broke off.

That foolish heart ducked back down beneath the covers. Her throat tightened.

Victor and Anika. They'd never even gotten to celebrate their first anniversary. Victor's private charter that had been flying them to a weekend getaway had crashed last October. There had been no survivors.

Justine still wondered if Anika had told Victor she was finally pregnant before they'd perished. She'd made herself believe that Anika had. A small thing but it had helped Justine in her grief, thinking how happy they'd been right to the end.

"It was a terrible thing," Stefan said. "I thought maybe I'd see you at their funeral."

She looked away from him and shook her head. None of them had been able to get to the funeral. Bad weather kept Todd and Debbie grounded in Minnesota. Garland had been in Japan for work.

And Justine—

"I couldn't go," she said thickly. *Please don't ask why. Not here. Not now. Not yet.*

Hillary returned with two folded towels in her

hand and Justine watched numbly as the woman crouched down again. Wiping up the rest of the spilled coffee with one. Wiping up Justine's foot and shin with the other.

She winced when Hillary got to her toe.

"Sorry, hon. Maybe hold the towel in place for a minute or two before you use a bandage." She set several bandage strips on the table. "Antiseptic ointment." She handed Justine another tiny foil packet.

Justine focused on the packet. So much easier than looking at Stefan's face.

The fact that he hadn't attempted to see her before the funeral was like a gong sounding inside her head. The noise was exceeded only by the gong of conscience that she hadn't tried to see him, either.

At least, not very hard.

That was *her* guilt.

Justine started when the stroller shook slightly and a bright yellow plastic doughnut-shaped toy flew out of it. She leaned over to catch the toy but it rolled out of her reach.

Bonita caught it without missing a beat. She set the pink bakery box she was carrying on Rebecca's table and twirled the toy around her finger.

Her attention was far more fixed on Stefan than it was on Justine. It was plainly obvious that Kirby's Perks' new barista found him attractive.

But then again, a woman would have to be buried six feet under not to find Stefan Mendoza attractive.

Justine leaned over to take care of her toe.

A cheerful burst of babbling from inside the stroller made her heart squeeze even more.

She tickled the baby's warm bare foot with her finger, earning a two-toothed smile in return.

She *should* have been more prepared.

Particularly after she'd seen Mark Mendoza right here in Kirby's Perks barely a week ago.

Stefan and Justine hadn't spent a lot of time talking about their families—she'd outright avoided talking about hers—but he had mentioned that they all lived in Austin. What he hadn't mentioned was that they looked like two peas in a pod.

At first glance, she'd thought Mark was Stefan. And the wedding ring on the hand he'd wrapped around his companion had made something inside her shrivel up and die.

But he hadn't been Stefan at all.

She should have known she wasn't really getting a reprieve.

Should have realized it was just a "coming attractions" preview.

She caught Bonita's eyes narrowing as they looked from Justine to Stefan and back again. "Do you two know each other?" she demanded.

Justine started to shake her head. "No, not, uh—"

"We met a while back," Stefan said. *He* hadn't looked away from Justine at all.

Bonita propped her hand on her curvy hip. She still had a smile on her face, but it had an edge now. Competitive vibes rolled off her. "A *while*?"

Justine felt an insane urge to laugh.

Hysteria.

Bonita was as gloriously beautiful as Stefan. Standing alongside each other—him in his narrow gray pants and white shirt with the sleeves rolled up and her with her poppy-red T-shirt and enviable curves—they looked perfectly suited for each other.

"Couple of years ago," Justine said. It was an exaggeration considering the more accurate seventeen months, but she didn't care. "In Florida."

At the table next to hers, Rebecca had closed her laptop and was looking at them, not making any secret of listening as she packed up her things. The writer had obviously finished her word count for the day. "Florida? I thought you moved here from Chatelaine."

Justine's skin felt hot. "I did. I was only visiting Miami. With my girlfriends from college."

"Ah, yes." Rebecca's eyes got a faraway look. "Even when I was young, spring break in Florida was de rigueur."

"It wasn't spring," Stefan said so abruptly it cleared the fog right out from Rebecca's expression.

After a moment, Rebecca gave Justine a smile that felt loaded with meaning. "Here." She pulled a parchment-wrapped muffin from her box and set it next to Justine's books. "I always buy too many for my critique group." Then she slung the strap of her bag over her shoulder. "Which I'm already running late for." She turned to leave.

Bonita touched Stefan's arm. "How'd the *colada* go over?"

"Fine." He still didn't look away from Justine. "I can't believe you're here."

"Same here," she managed huskily. The yellow doughnut-shaped toy was followed by an orange one that hit her squarely in her chest. She caught it automatically.

Stefan's gaze finally released hers. He looked down at the stroller.

She saw the twitch in his left eyebrow. The one with the small rakish scar that made perfection look even more perfect.

Then, seeming to forget Bonita altogether, he slowly walked around the table that Rebecca had vacated. And even more slowly circled the stroller until he could see beneath the big navy canopy with the stylish khaki polka dots.

The baby boy was dressed in dinosaur-printed shorts and a T-shirt with Mommy's Favorite Dude printed across the front.

His olive-toned skin was flawlessly smooth, and his dark hair was already thick and curled over his forehead. He had two little teeth, white as snow in his open-mouthed smile, and eyes as green as soft moss.

Stefan's jaw tightened until a whitish line formed.

He didn't say a word as he crouched in front of the baby.

His baby.

He reached out a hand and Justine started, then

swallowed whatever sound she'd been going to make at the look he gave her. Sharp and hard as emeralds. But the thumb he stroked over the baby's cheek was gentle. "He's my son."

She trembled. Yes, her son was the spitting image of his father. But how could Stefan not even *question* the truth? Maybe once the initial surprise passed, he would. Maybe he'd want a DNA test.

Maybe even require one.

Bonita slapped the plastic toy down on Justine's table. "How old is he?" She wore a decidedly suspicious look.

"Eight months," Stefan answered before Justine could.

"To the day," she added huskily. Not for Bonita's sake but for his.

Bonita stomped back to the counter, tossing her apron aside. "I'm going on a break," she snapped at Hillary and disappeared into the back room.

Bonita was the least of Justine's concerns.

Stefan unclipped the stroller's safety harness.

"He doesn't like strangers," she warned quickly.

"I'm his father," he said tightly. "I shouldn't be a stranger." He finished lifting out the baby and straightened. Green eyes met green eyes. "What's his name?"

The knot was growing in her chest. She cleared her throat. "Morgan."

Stefan looked startled and the baby suddenly squirmed and let out an ear-piercing wail as he reached for Justine. Her hands brushed Stefan's as she quickly took the baby. Her son immediately stopped wailing and smiled through the huge teardrops clinging to his lush black eyelashes.

He patted her cheek and babbled charmingly.

"You should have told me." Stefan's voice was flat.

Justine lifted her chin. Morgan's solid weight in her arms was a comfort. She was a good mother. That didn't justify her silence about his birth, but during their time together in Florida, Stefan had never suggested pursuing *anything* after he'd left her hotel suite. They hadn't shared life stories. They definitely hadn't shared phone numbers or email addresses. "I never expected to see you again."

"I told you I'd moved to Austin. You didn't say a word that you were from Texas."

She had no defense for that. She hadn't told him about Chatelaine because—for that brief New Year's weekend a year and a half ago—she'd wanted to be someone other than the virgin from Chatelaine. "It's a big state." Her voice shook.

His lips thinned and he pulled out his cell phone and frowned at it for a while before he started swiping the screen. "I'm calling my lawyer."

Her chair screeched as she backed away, automatically turning aside to shield Morgan. "You're not taking him from me!"

He swore impatiently. "I'm not trying to. But I need to make certain he's provided for."

She lifted her chin even higher. Even before she'd decided to study social work, she'd known how the system operated. "Just because I don't have a lot of money doesn't mean I'm not providing for my son."

"Our son," he corrected and cast a look around them when the door opened again.

A crowd of women wearing yoga togs streamed in, their laughter loud.

He raked his fingers through his hair before pointing at her cell phone where it sat on the table. "What's your phone number?"

Feeling shaky inside, she told him. He dialed it, but when her phone remained silent, he gave her a look. "Don't lie."

Her teeth set on edge. She snatched up the phone. "I *don't* lie." She showed him the screen with a phone number displaying the incoming call. "I *do* however, observe the courtesy of keeping my phone silenced when I'm in someone's place of business!"

He didn't look the least chastised when he pocketed his phone. "I'll call you later," he said. He reached out to wiggle Morgan's bare foot and the baby shied away from him again. His gaze captured Justine's and held. "When I do, *answer.*"

She didn't quite have the nerve to call him out for sounding so high-handed and felt like a total wimp as she silently watched him sidle through the crowd of customers and push through the door.

But what else *should* she do?

Run after him with explanations that suddenly felt very thin and paltry?

She'd known his name. Until Victor's plane went down, she'd had a means to find him.

But she hadn't.

Oh, she'd tried looking him up in Austin once. There'd been about two hundred Mendozas but no Stefan Mendoza.

Then she'd slept off the lone glass of champagne she'd allowed herself last New Year's Eve and hadn't looked again.

"You okay there, Justine?"

She sank down weakly into her chair, hugging Morgan tightly to her. Annette was giving her a concerned look.

"I'm okay," she managed.

Now *that* was a lie.

Annette glanced at the counter where Bonita had returned to help Hillary with the crush of customers, then scooted her chair over to Justine's table. She lowered her voice. "Since I quit working here to help out at my dad's office, I know Kirby has needed more help than just Hillary. But seriously. She was scraping the bottom of the barrel with Bonita. She flirts with every guy who comes in."

"I'm sure she's fine," Justine defended even though she'd noticed the same thing. She just hadn't cared before Bonita turned her attention on Stefan.

"I bet she wouldn't say the same thing about you,"

Annette said under her breath. "So that guy Stefan is really Morgan's—"

"Yes," Justine said abruptly.

Annette toyed with the thick silver ring on her thumb. "In all the time you've been coming in here, you've never talked about him."

"There was nothing to talk about," Justine said. Beneath the edgy drama of her heavy black eyeliner and black clothes, Annette was a tender soul. "I never expected to see him again, much less here—" Her throat closed again.

Annette leaned closer, dropping her voice even more. "Was he married?"

"No!"

Morgan threw the toys across the table again and squirmed in her lap. He was hardly ever fussy, but when she was upset, he usually picked up on it.

It was one of the reasons she'd left Chatelaine and moved to Rambling Rose. She'd managed to stay under her mother's roof with Morgan for all of two weeks before she'd known she had to leave. It had taken her another two weeks to find somewhere to live that she could afford and then it had only come about because Debbie's aunt in Rambling Rose needed a new tenant for her garage apartment.

The yoga crowd was starting to commandeer the tables around her and Annette.

"I need to get going." She tucked Morgan inside the stroller and gathered up the scattered toys. She stowed them along with her textbooks in the cargo area below the seat.

"Don't forget the muffin," Annette reminded, noisily sucking the straw of her nearly empty cup. "And I need to get back to the office, too."

Even though Justine was far less interested in bran muffins than Rebecca thought everyone should be, she wrapped it in a napkin and tucked it in her backpack that doubled as a diaper bag before steering the stroller out of the shop. Annette tossed her cup in the trash as she followed.

The afternoon sun was still hot and high in the sky.

"Want a ride?"

Justine shook her head. "The walk will help me clear my head." She hung her backpack off the handle since it was just too hot to wear it herself. "Thanks though."

"You know," Annette said, "if you ever want to talk or…or something…"

Justine managed a smile. "I appreciate that." She took a step away, then stopped. For months, they'd forged a sort of little group as Kirby's regulars. Annette and Rebecca. Martin and Justine. The Friday four. And nearly every other day, too. Aside from their loyalty to Kirby's Perks, Justine and Martin had bonded over their shared interest in collecting postcards and Rebecca had started dropping hints that Annette ought to try her hand at writing children's books. "Have you heard anything about Martin?"

"I visited him at the hospital earlier this week. He was pretty out of it. Rambling like he was still a kid. I thought maybe he knew who I was, but then he started calling me Annie, which he never used to do. The nurse came in to take him for some tests so I didn't stay long." She smiled sadly. "He wasn't happy about the tests but he calmed down when the nurse gave him one of the postcards *you'd* sent him. So at least he hasn't seemed to have forgotten that he collects the things, same as you."

Instead of making Justine feel better, it just made her feel worse. He'd been hospitalized for more than a week now and all she'd done was mail a couple of postcards that she'd thought he would like. "I'll make a point of getting over to visit him. Has anyone found out what's wrong?"

Annette fiddled with the spiky choker around her neck as she shook her head. "Never thought I'd say it, but I miss him being around. Spouting off his opinions whether anyone wants them or not. I know he always said he didn't have any family, but if you'd have heard the way he talked while I was at the hospital?" She lifted her thin shoulder. "It must not have always been that way."

"Families don't always stick together," Justine murmured.

A vintage pickup truck slowed on the street next to them and the middle-aged woman behind the wheel waved cheerfully at them as she drove past.

"And sometimes families just crop up out of nowhere," Annette said under her breath. Then she gave Justine a swift look of regret. "I didn't mean about Morgan's father. Just, you know—Mariana there finding out she's related to the Fortune family."

Mariana—and the flea-market she'd founded— was a fixture in Rambling Rose. And the news about her and the Fortunes had fueled gossip in and out of the coffee shop for weeks. Not least because the Fortunes were—mostly—very well off and figured prominently in the town's steep economic rise, but because the discovery had apparently been shrouded with odd little mysteries like anonymous gifts and secret safe-deposit boxes.

"I heard Mariana did a DNA test and everything," Annette said. Then she smiled impishly. "My mom did one of those DNA kits they sell online? Now she gets emails all the time about how she has some new third cousin twice removed in Europe."

Justine forced a smile, which was what she knew Annette intended, even though she really couldn't think about DNA tests without thinking about Stefan.

"All the Fortunes I've met have been nice," she said now. "Particularly Josh." He was Kirby's new fiancé. "If you ask me, they're even more fortunate to add Mariana to their ranks."

"My folks took me out to the market every weekend when I was a kid. Mariana always gave me a treat from her food truck. She's a sweetheart for sure." Annette jingled her skull-shaped key chain. "Are you *sure* I can't drive you?"

"I'm sure." Justine's garage apartment was only a few blocks. "You don't have a car seat. And your dad's office is the other direction."

Annette smile turned rueful. "You saying that my coffee break has gone on too long?" She jingled her keys again and set off. "See you later."

Justine pushed her sunglasses onto her nose and let her smile die as she turned toward home.

The oversize wheels of the fancy stroller easily rolled over the sidewalk that got increasingly uneven the closer she got to home. Rambling Rose was a growing community with new businesses and new homes going up all over. But this was the area of town where the houses were timeworn and settled. Where yards were small and mostly unfenced. Where driveways were narrow and unpaved as often as not.

It really wasn't any different than where she'd grown up in Chatelaine.

Would Stefan find the neighborhood wanting?

Her fingers tightened around the handle, and she walked faster. Which only earned a stubbed toe on the already injured digit when her sandal caught on a raised lip of cement.

Tears sprang to her eyes and she wanted to cry. She fumbled in her backpack for a tissue and the muffin rolled onto the ground.

She sniffled and picked it up.

What Stefan thought was immaterial.

Because Justine didn't really care what the neighborhood looked like. The neighbors were friendly and waved when they saw you on the street and didn't look at you with pity or judgment in their eyes.

And they gave you muffins, not because they felt sorry for you, but because it was just their nature to be kind.

She tucked away the muffin and wiped her cheeks. She wiggled her toe.

Sore, but not broken.

Morgan had fallen asleep and she started walking again, passing two more houses before turning up the driveway where she lived.

A late-model SUV took up most of the way.

Her landlord was having a lot of visitors these days. Ever since she'd gotten home from her last vacation. Justine needed to remember to mention it to Debbie the next time they talked. Debbie would be glad to know her widowed aunt's social life was alive and well.

At the end of the narrow driveway was an equally narrow garage with an exterior staircase leading up to Justine's one-bedroom apartment. Morgan was so sound he didn't wake up when she lifted him out of the stroller.

She carried him upstairs and settled him in the crib that her four brothers had pooled together to give her when he was born. She gulped down a glass of water, then went back downstairs again. She unloaded her books and the backpack and stored the stroller in the closet-sized space that Gwen had allotted her beneath the staircase. It had probably been meant at one point to store bicycles or lawn mowers. It wasn't gorgeous but it was weather tight and fit not only enormous baby gear but a few other essentials as well.

She glanced at her little economy car that was parked in the alley behind the garage. The back tire that she'd filled with air the other day still looked full.

Thankfully. She didn't want to add a new tire to her already lean budget.

She shouldered the backpack and took the books in her arm and went back up the stairs again. There was a tiny landing at the top. Just enough to hold a plastic lawn chair without blocking the door. She paused next to it and looked around.

In the yard next door, a couple of children were squealing as they ran back and forth through a sprinkler. A few houses over, someone was mowing their lawn.

It was just an ordinary summer afternoon. Like the afternoon yesterday had been. Like the afternoon tomorrow would be.

Only nothing was ordinary anymore.

Because Stefan Mendoza was no longer just a memory that still kept her warm at night.

He was *here*.

In all his Mr. Perfect glory.

Chapter Three

Mr. Perfect didn't follow through with the threatened phone call, though. Justine's phone stayed silent the rest of the day.

Morgan woke from his nap cranky and famished. Fortunately, the famished part was easily solved, which had the added benefit of solving the crankiness, too. When she checked the screen of her cell phone for the third time in just an hour, annoyance with herself had her sticking the phone in a drawer. The worst of the day's heat was already abating so she strapped Morgan into the baby carrier that had been a gift from Debbie and Todd and walked to the park.

It wasn't large. Just a few benches next to a set

of swings and a climbing structure with a tunnel-type slide. At that hour while most people were sitting down at the dinner table, they had the place to themselves.

They played in the sandbox and then Morgan scooted around in the grass to chase his favorite grabby ball and when he tired of that, she popped him in one of the baby-sized swings while he squealed in delight.

By that time, the sun was descending, and she donned the carrier once again. She'd used the thing almost exclusively for the first six months because she hadn't been able to bring herself to unbox the luxury stroller. It had been a gift from Anika and Victor.

But it had arrived a week after they'd died.

A week after Justine gave birth.

She hadn't been able to look at it without being swamped with grief.

Back at the apartment, she took the phone out of the drawer again. Stefan still had not called.

Was she relieved? Or worried?

She plugged in the phone to charge while she fed and bathed Morgan. Then they sat in the rocking chair that she'd found secondhand out at Mariana's Market. She nursed him and they read a couple of board books—mostly an exercise that involved snuggling him while he turned the pages back and forth and babbled—and when he started rubbing his eyes, she tucked him in his crib again.

He turned onto his stomach, stuck his thumb in his mouth and his butt up in the air and was asleep in minutes. She knew from having spent endless hours watching him that he'd abandon the thumb after just a few minutes and then he'd sleep the next twelve hours nearly straight.

She would have been happy to sit there silently adoring him now, too, except she had deadlines to meet.

She pulled the bedroom door almost closed and went back into the living area. She could see the light flashing on her phone from across the room telling her she'd missed a call and her stomach lurched.

But when she picked it up to look at the screen, it wasn't Stefan who'd called but a telemarketer.

She deleted the voice mail and opened her laptop. She was still trying to finish her schooling, but she paid the bills by working as a virtual assistant. Currently, she had half a dozen clients, doing everything from bookkeeping to managing their social media accounts.

By the time she handled the day's tasks, it was after midnight.

She took a break long enough to refill her empty coffee mug and check on Morgan. He'd been sleeping through the night for the last week, which meant she now had a plentiful supply of breast milk in her freezer because her body was still prepared for him to wake up and need feeding. While she pumped and listened to the water gurgling through the coffee filter, she answered her personal emails—mostly from Garland who was in Japan once again.

She wasn't sure exactly why she didn't tell Garland about encountering Stefan again, but it nagged her through two cups of coffee and the two chapters she had to read for her online class.

Except for constantly rehashing those moments in the coffee shop, it was a routine night for Justine. Usually when she climbed into bed about three in the morning, she went right to sleep.

But not this time.

This time, she tossed and turned, reliving every moment she'd spent with Stefan in Florida until light was creeping around the edges of the blinds hanging in the bedroom window.

Morgan woke her.

She dragged herself out of bed and plucked him from the crib. She changed his soaked diaper, turned on the morning news and sat down to nurse him again. Then she set him on his favorite blanket on the living room floor with a few toys and fixed some breakfast for them both. He was rocking back and forth on his knees, chattering like a magpie at the news anchor when she moved him to his high chair.

When she tried to feed him some rice cereal, he clamped his mouth shut and tried turning nearly all the way around in his chair.

"Sure." She kissed the top of his curls. "Stop eating this right after I've bought a new box of it." She moved the bowl away from him and dropped some dry snack puffs on his tray. They were more for entertainment than sustenance, but she'd learned that feeding a cooperative Morgan was a lot easier than feeding a noncooperative one. And along with sleeping through the night, he'd also decided recently that the only things he wanted to eat were foods that were orange.

While he plowed his fingers through his food, she picked up her phone. If she didn't want to sit around worrying when Stefan was going to contact her, there was one solution. Take control of the small thing that she could control.

You can see Morgan today between his naps. Between 10 and 1 should be good.

Before she could talk herself out of it, she sent the text message. Then she coaxed Morgan into tasting her oatmeal.

He made a face and spit it right back out, with a huge smile that had her laughing despite the mess.

She wiped him up, gave him a few more puffs and pulled out the carrots that she'd cooked the night before. "You're going to turn orange at this rate."

"Nananana!" He pounced on the small bits, mashing as many as he managed to pinch between his fingers. She snuck in a few spoonsful of cottage cheese she'd mixed with butternut squash from a baby food pouch.

It looked appalling, but the mixture met his latest color requirement, so he gobbled it down.

She wiped him up again and put him down to play while she set the kitchen to rights. When she heard the distinctive *ping* of a text message, she nearly knocked over her glass of milk grabbing for the phone.

Address?

Feeling ridiculously nervous, she sent her answer.

Then she sat on the floor with Morgan. While he stacked blocks and then gleefully knocked them down, she snatched looks at the next chapter she needed to read. The words were just collections of letters on a page though.

She was too preoccupied by Stefan.

She ended up tossing the book aside and stretched out on the floor next to Morgan and played with him until naptime. As soon as he was asleep, she took a shower and tried to convince herself that she wasn't taking extra care with her appearance.

Sure, she wore lip gloss every day of the week when it was just her and Morgan.

Naturally, she wore her best paisley sundress when all she had on the schedule was crawling around on the floor with her sweet boy, chasing the toys that he'd discovered were so much fun to throw.

And of course, she always fussed with her hair for a solid half hour, making sure she had just the right combination of height and sleekness to her ponytail that she'd possessed for a particular Florida New Year's Eve.

She didn't own a full-length mirror. Instead, she stood barefoot on the closed toilet lid and turned this way and that, examining her reflection in a too-small mirror over the sink.

Yesterday, Stefan had caught her unaware.

Not today. Today, she looked as good as she could look.

And at least Garland and Debbie weren't around to deem her sundress as frumpy as the party dress they'd nixed a year and a half ago.

She climbed down from the toilet and slid her feet into platform flip-flops that were fancy only because of the sparkly daisies over the toes.

Morgan woke after an hour with his usual sunny disposition.

She fed him again and was just changing him into a plaid romper when she heard a knock on her door.

Though she'd taken the bull by the horns by texting Stefan, her nerves still shot into orbit.

She picked up Morgan and buried her nose in his sweet neck. Everything that was important was wrapped up in her son. "It's all going to be fine," she told him shakily.

He chattered at her and tugged at her hair, dislodging her painstaking work on the ponytail.

The knock came at the door again and rather than try to fix her hair, she just yanked the holder out altogether. Pretending that her knees didn't feel mushy, she went to open the door.

No amount of preparation kept her stomach from hollowing at the sight of Stefan standing on her doorstep. He wore dark blue jeans and a stark white Henley. His dark hair was slicked back as much as the thick, wavy strands could be slicked, and sunglasses shielded his green eyes.

A yellow gift bag patterned with zoo animals dangled from his fingers.

He seemed no more certain what to say in greeting than she did.

Morgan was no help, either.

He took one look at Stefan and immediately buried his head shyly against Justine's shoulder.

"Here." Stefan finally held out the gift bag.

It broke the ice.

She took the bag and jiggled it temptingly in front of Morgan. "Come in."

Morgan wasn't tempted by the bag. He eyed it suspiciously while Justine eyed Stefan, watching for any sign of disapproval as he entered the small apartment.

Her living room was scrupulously clean and only a little untidy thanks to the blocks she just now spotted lurking beneath the edge of the couch.

If he noticed them, he didn't show it. Instead, he seemed focused on the wall above her couch. "That's a lot of postcards."

"I've collected them since I was a kid." She'd

made a collage out of a batch, gluing them to an art canvas that she'd bought for pennies at the same booth where she'd gotten her rocking chair. Now the area above her couch was awash in vibrant hues. "At least this way they're not sitting unused in a box just taking up space." When every inch of storage space was at a premium, a person had to get creative.

"I like it."

He was being polite. Like someone who needed to be on their best behavior.

So was she.

"Have a seat." She gestured at the couch. More secondhand furniture that she'd covered herself. It wasn't perfect, but the slipcover hid the comfy but ancient upholstery beneath, with the added benefit that she could wash it when she needed to.

He sat on one end of the couch. She sat on the other and held Morgan on her lap.

The only thing that saved the awkward silence from being excruciating was Morgan. His curiosity about the gift bag was finally outweighing his shyness. Only instead of looking inside the bag, he was trying to bite the glossy paper.

"It's nothing much." Stefan rubbed his palm over his thigh. "I just saw it in the store."

She'd never seen Stefan wear jeans before. And if that wasn't a testament to the brevity of their— what did she call it? *Friendship* didn't fit. Nor did *relationship*.

Fantasy?

Heat gathered under her skin and she quickly directed Morgan's attention to the tissue paper.

It was hard to pretend nonchalance when her emotions felt so tangled.

This is your first gift from your daddy!

No amount of effort would shove the thought to the side.

All she ended up with was a tight throat and an alarming prickling sensation behind her eyes.

Her emotions hadn't felt this out of control since she'd been pregnant.

She bounced Morgan on her knee and stared at the faded area rug under their feet. "Did you have any trouble finding our address?"

"No. How long have you lived here?"

"Since November." She pressed her lips together for a moment. "You told me you and your brothers all lived in Austin." She heard the accusatory tone and winced. Twenty-four years old and already sounding like her mother whenever Kimberly made some reference to her children's father. Rick Maloney had been absent ever since she'd become pregnant with Justine. After four kids before her, he had been done. Done, done, done.

He'd left them and their home in Chatelaine and never come back.

"We did all live in Austin," Stefan said evenly. "Whereas you didn't tell me much of anything at all. Do you want to debate who was less forthcoming?"

Her chest felt tight. Morgan finally pulled the tissue out of the bag and watched it float toward the floor, caught in the stream of air blowing from the air conditioner. He scrambled off her knee, prepared to follow it headfirst and she set his feet on the floor. He held onto the side of the couch and bounced a few times before sitting down on his butt with a plop. Then he turned over and scooted on his belly with one knee sort of lifting in his half version of a crawl, after the tissue paper. Once he caught it, the thin paper was doomed.

Justine got up and gathered the shredded remains before Morgan could try to eat any of it. She distracted him with the gift bag and returned to her corner of the couch. This time, she rehearsed the words—and tone—in her head. "What brought you to Rambling Rose?"

Stefan leaned forward and clasped his hands loosely between his knees. "My brothers Mark and Rodrigo moved to Rambling Rose a while back and—"

"So, you're just visiting—"

"No. I moved here, too. Last month. I'll be remodeling a place I bought just outside town."

"Why?" All her frustration where the ironies of the universe were concerned was bound in the single word.

Morgan ripped a corner of the gift bag off and a set of oversize toy keys fell out. He pounced on them and waved them over his head.

"Success," Stefan murmured. He held out his

hand toward Morgan, but the baby ignored him and scooted farther away with the keys clenched in his hand.

"It's not you." Justine got up to shut the bedroom door, cutting off Morgan's only escape route. His scoot-crawl method might not look particularly textbook, but it was effective and fast. "It's all str—"

"Yeah, I know." Stefan's fingers clawed through his hair. "Strangers." He exhaled and linked his fingers together again. His layer of calm might be sturdier than hers, but it seemed just as hard-won. "Well, here we are. In Rambling Rose of all places. You told the woman in the coffee shop yesterday that you were from Chatelaine."

She perched on the stool at her breakfast bar. "It's a couple hours north of here."

"I looked it up."

She chewed the inside of her cheek. "When we were in Florida, we didn't…didn't get into personal stuff."

"Telling me you were sick of being a virgin felt pretty personal."

"You know what I mean." She hopped back off the stool, but she couldn't outrun the memory of telling him exactly that. They'd been salsa dancing at Victor's club. Her in another borrowed dress that was cut up to here and down to there and she'd been stone cold sober at the time.

Stefan had just laughed and asked her how old she was before escorting her back off the dance floor.

He'd told her he never played with amateurs and disappeared after that, and she'd believed it was for good.

The next afternoon when he'd knocked on her hotel room door and asked her to lunch, she'd been stunned.

She pushed away the vivid memories and stared out the window next to the front door. The driveway was full up with three late model SUV's. If one of them belonged to Stefan, she hoped he wasn't blocked in by her landlady's visitors. "It was just a fling." For some reason, the term sounded less damning than *one-night stand*.

"That doesn't mean you shouldn't have told me."

"Yeah, because that's what every guy wants to hear months down the road. 'Hey there! Remember that one time in Florida? Guess what? Condoms *aren't* a-hundred-percent effective.'" She turned away from the window and looked at him. "Morgan was hardly planned but he's my—"

"Don't say responsibility," Stefan cut in, looking annoyed. "He's *not* just your responsibility."

World, she thought. She'd been going to say that Morgan was her world. And her world was presently pulling on the hem of her sundress so hard that the stretchy neckline was in danger of exposing her nursing bra.

She reached down and unlatched his grip before picking him up and yanking the top of her dress back in place.

"And that's why there's just one thing to do." Stefan rose from the couch and suddenly seemed to take up even more than his fair share of the small apartment.

He'd probably gone straight from the coffee shop the day before to consult the lawyer he'd threatened. It didn't mean things needed to turn adversarial. Particularly if she took the offensive. "Obviously, I won't deny that you're Morgan's father, so I think the best thing to do is—"

"You need to marry me."

"What?" Shock vibrated through her as his words sank in. "Have you lost your senses?"

"Children benefit from two parents and—"

"Two parents who both want to be parents in the first place!" She'd closed the bedroom door on Morgan, but she was the one who felt like there was no escape. "And what's the rule these days that says those parents have to be *married*?"

His eyes narrowed. "Generations of tradition?"

She snorted. "Didn't work for my parents."

"Didn't work for mine either," he said without missing a beat. "I'm not suggesting a real marriage. But even if it's platonic, the legality of one protects us all!"

"I don't care *what* sort of marriage you're talking about." She was horrified by a stab of secret longing and felt behind her for the doorknob of the front door.

"Where the hell are you going?"

"I need some air." She was squeezing Morgan so

tightly he squawked in protest. She stepped out on the landing and pounded down the stairs and set him on Gwen's tidily mown rear lawn.

Stefan followed.

She threw up her hand, staving him off. She couldn't think straight when he got too near. "Don't."

He frowned and spread his hands. "Don't *what*, Justine? Do the right thing?"

Her laugh sounded desperate even to her own ears. "This is *soooo* not the right thing!" She tucked her hair behind both ears and paced to the chain-link fence separating Gwen's yard from the neighbor's.

"I'm his father. I want the rights of a father!"

"I'm not trying to stop you." She paced back, only to feel breathless when she neared him, and she turned on her sparkly flip-flops and headed to the fence. "We don't have to get married for you to be Morgan's father. You *are* his father."

"Not legally," he said through his teeth. "Not in Texas. The law doesn't work that way here."

"Then we'll file an Acknowledgment of Paternity stating that you *are* his father."

"What about custody? Visitation? All of that? I'm not going to be a part-time father," Stefan said flatly. "Someone you pull out when it's convenient for you."

"I never suggested that."

"An AOP and marriage is the perfect solution. I want my family to know him and for him to know them."

She pinched the bridge of her nose. If her mother

had felt similarly, Justine and Morgan would still be in Chatelaine and none of this would be happening.

And then she felt a sharp pang for even thinking it. Because Morgan did deserve a father. A *present* father.

Something she'd never had.

She cleared her throat. "I'm willing to work out some sort of…of…arrangement—"

"Generous."

"—but not marriage."

The side door of the main house opened, and a group of people exited. Gwen waved toward her. "Yoohoo, Justine! Isn't it a *glorious* day?"

Glorious wouldn't be Justine's word choice. But she returned Gwen's wave with one of her own.

With a slam of vehicle doors, Gwen's guests began departing.

Clearly, none of the SUV's belonged to Stefan.

When the driveway was vacated, Gwen looked their way again. "Come over later, dear. There's so much to chat about."

To Gwendolyn Meyers, a chat could mean anything from laughter-filled gab sessions to late-night poignant reminiscences about her late husband.

At the moment, Justine was more interested in keeping Gwen from walking over. "I will," she called back. Her landlady was a dear soul who rented the apartment to Justine for a song. Gwen wasn't shocked and disappointed by the fact that Justine was a single mother. She didn't make unrelenting comments about Justine's "regrettable state" or refer to Morgan as her worst mistake.

Justine was nevertheless relieved when the woman disappeared into her house once more.

Stefan extracted something from his wallet and extended his hand. "Take it."

"I don't need your credit card." She had one of her own. It had a modest limit and she tried hard never to use it.

"It's not my credit card. It's yours. I set up the account yesterday for Morgan's expenses."

"No, thank you." She folded her arms pointedly. "If Morgan needs something, I provide it. I *have* provided it."

His lips thinned again. "I'm not saying you haven't."

"One of the reasons I chose Rambling Rose was because of the new pediatric center here. Morgan's at the top of the growth charts and hits every developmental milestone. He's fed and safe and loved."

Most importantly, he was loved. Unquestionably, unequivocally loved. From the moment she'd realized she was pregnant, she'd wanted him.

Stefan's brows were pulled together. "Who made you so defensive, Justine? Have I questioned *any* of that?" He waved his hand at Morgan. The baby had abandoned the play keys in favor of a twig and was banging it on the ground. "I have perfectly good vision. I can see he's thriving."

"I'm not defensive," she muttered. Proving, of course, that she most definitely *was*.

And Stefan had the nerve to flash an unexpected smile.

He quickly wiped it away, but she'd still seen it.

She hauled in a deep breath and let it out slowly. That smile was partly responsible for the very reason why she couldn't afford to still be swayed by it.

No matter how seductively tempting it might be.

She was a grown woman. She paid her bills— almost always on time—and just because the only man she'd ever slept with was standing three feet away from her suggesting marriage didn't mean she should agree.

She didn't have to do anything she didn't want to. Such as apologize every minute of every day to her own mother for the course of her life.

"Justine."

That was all he said. Her name. And she was suddenly remembering the way he'd whispered her name when he'd undressed her as if he'd been uncovering something extraordinary…

"Please. Just take it."

She blinked hard and leaned over to take the credit card he was still extending. She was extremely careful not to touch him in the process. "I'm never going to use it," she warned huskily.

"That's up to you. But I am going to be part of my son's life. That's not up for negotiation."

"What do you want me to do?" She sounded more flippant than she felt. "Text you when it's time to change his diaper?"

"It'd be a helluva lot more than you've offered in the last seventeen months." His voice was tight.

Her conscience pinched. Hard. "I usually take him to the park before I feed him his supper. After that it's bath time and getting him ready for bed. It's the longest stretch of the day when he's awake if you want to come by then."

"Where's the park?"

She told him.

He nodded and went down on one knee next to Morgan. "See you later, buddy," he said softly.

Morgan banged his stick a few times, his green eyes looking from Stefan to Justine and back again. He didn't shrink away from Stefan exactly, but his expression was plainly wary.

Stefan obviously recognized that fact because he didn't try to get closer.

"Let me know if your plans change," he told Justine as he straightened. "Otherwise, I'll see you at the park."

Then without a backward glance, he walked away.

Chapter Four

"What do you mean, you've got a son?"

He was in Costa Rica, but Esteban Mendoza's voice was as clear through Stefan's phone as if he was standing next to him.

"Just that." Stefan climbed onto a large boulder and squinted at the landscape around him. Thanks to a ready source of water from the creek that ran through his property and Adam's adjacent one, the grassland was greener than some places. Not as green as Florida but he was getting used to it. "His name is Morgan. He's eight months old."

"Are you sure he's yours?"

Stefan's shoulders tightened, but he knew his father's intentions were good. "He's mine."

"And his mama?"

"Her name's Justine Maloney." Her image filled his brain way too easily. Her smile. Her eyes. The way her breath had hitched when she'd reached for his belt—

He pinched his eyes closed in a pointless attempt to staunch the flow of erotic memories. "We met that time I visited you in Miami at New Year's. I was negotiating with Victor Montenegro—"

"I remember. You never mentioned a woman. I'm guessing it was just a hookup? Didn't I teach you to be more careful than that?"

He wasn't often irritated with his father. He dropped his hand. "It wasn't a hookup."

"Then what was it?"

A hookup.

And so much more. She was the woman he'd been measuring everyone against ever since.

And now, knowing that they had a child together?

"I thought we *were* careful." Stefan hopped down from the boulder and started toward the house.

"So what do you intend to do about it?"

"Be a father! I told her we should get married."

"Learn from my history, son. Give that another thought. Then another twenty more after that."

Esteban's one and only marriage might have been impetuous, but it had produced five of his six sons before it had ended. Now Esteban freely admitted that Stefan's mother had been right to leave. They'd been much better parents singly than they had ever been jointly.

Which didn't help Stefan's argument where Justine was concerned in the slightest. "She hasn't accepted yet." Talk about marketing spin. He changed the subject. "When are you coming back from Costa Rica? And is it true that you took Mrs. Shevchenko with you?"

"She just wanted to stir the coals under the fella she's been dating. Worked, too. She's already back in Miami planning her next set of nuptials. Maybe she'll ask me to give her away," Esteban said on a chuckle. "Anyway, figure I'll be back home in a week or so. Guess I'll head your way to meet my new grandson soon enough. Morgan, you say?"

"Yeah." Stefan rubbed his chin.

"Good name," Esteban said. "Solid. Remember Morgan's in Little Havana?"

The place was indelibly etched in Stefan's mind. He didn't believe it was a coincidence that Justine had named their child for the restaurant he'd taken her to before they'd ended up in bed together. "I remember."

"Send me a picture of him."

If he'd needed evidence that discovering Morgan had thrown him for a loop, the fact that he hadn't yet taken a picture of the baby would be plenty. "I will."

"Might think about turning one of those bedrooms in your new place into a room for the baby.

And while you're at it, forget thinking about ways you can sell Justine on marriage."

Stefan was used to his father's ability to tune in to his train of thought. "I'm not trying to *sell* her on anything," he denied anyway.

"Sure you're not," Esteban scoffed. "Maybe instead of focusing on getting what you want, you should focus on what she needs. Let *her* set the pace. Do you have a clue what sort of demands a baby brings to the day? What other kind of help does she have? Her ma? A babysitter? Daycare? What does she do when she's at work?"

Stefan rubbed his chin again. Aside from knowing Justine was still a student, he didn't really know squat.

Other than she came from Chatelaine.

Big deal. From what he'd seen when he'd looked it up, the town was stuck in the past the way that Rambling Rose had been until a few years ago. Now property values in his new hometown were on the rise, and construction was going on all over the place as people left Houston and Austin for its small-town appeal.

Chatelaine didn't appear as lucky.

"I don't know what she does," he admitted.

His father's silence was telling. "Send that pic, son, and we'll catch up soon as I'm back in the States."

Stefan didn't have a chance to pocket his phone

before it rang again. Adam's number was as familiar as his own. He answered. "What's up?"

"Larkin's running a fever." Adam's voice was terse. "We're taking him to Houston to see his transplant doctor just to be safe. Laurel's getting him in the car now."

Stefan was startled. "It's that serious?"

"Every fever is still serious. Thank God they're rare. His usual pediatrician wants to be cautious."

"Yeah. Always." Stefan hadn't been in Rambling Rose two years ago, but Adam had filled him in about the community-wide search for a bone marrow donor for the seemingly abandoned infant. Learning he was a donor match hadn't been as shocking as learning he was the boy's father and the subsequent discovery that Larkin's mother, Laurel, was suffering from amnesia in another state. Even though Laurel had recovered and they'd been reunited as a family, Adam didn't take anything for granted.

"Just focus on your family," Stefan said. "Do what you need. I have things covered here. I'll reschedule the zoning guy." Adam was supposed to be meeting him that afternoon.

"Don't reschedule. It took weeks to get the appointment set. All he needs is to see the plans, but we need that final rubber stamp."

"I'll take care of it." He had a copy of the plans, too. "Let me know how things go when you can."

"Will do." Adam ended the call.

Stefan rubbed his face. Justine had said she and

Morgan would be at the park at four. But he couldn't be there if he was at the brewery site meeting with the zoning commissioner.

He started to send her a text message but hit the call button instead.

She answered on the third ring. "I had it on Silent," she said in greeting. "Morgan's sleeping."

In other words, send text messages when the baby sleeps. "I won't be able to make it to the park."

"Okay," she said after half a beat that he wasn't even sure had been half a beat at all.

Maybe it was his imagination. Conjuring conflict just because he expected it.

He pushed through the back door of the house, leaving the hot sunshine behind for the cool, dim interior of a kitchen straight out of the sixties. "I have to meet a guy from the zoning commission."

"Fine. Whatever."

Definitely *not* his imagination.

"I'll be there as soon as I finish." His dad's words hovered in his head. "I'll bring dinner," he added abruptly.

Her hesitation this time was a lot longer. Her "Fine" even more clipped.

So far, he was doing a helluva job of things.

"Any preference? Allergies?"

"Include something orange," she said. "But not actual oranges. He's too young for oranges." Then she hung up on him.

He squinted at the avocado-green appliances that

dominated his dated kitchen. What was orange besides pumpkins and carrots? Both of which he hated.

Fortunately, he had an idea who could help…

He called Ashley and before he could even fill in
his sister-in-law about the situation, she told him that
she'd just heard the news from his dad. "You *have*
to bring Justine and the baby by Provisions. We all
want to meet them!"

"I'll think about it. Right now, she's not overjoyed
to find I'm here, much less subjecting her to half my
whole family."

"Half? Please. It takes weddings to bring out half
of your whole family."

"I could say the same about the Fortunes." The
massive New Year's Eve wedding when Mark and
Megan had gotten married—along with four other
members of the extensive Fortune family—was still
fresh in Stefan's mind. And it served as a stellar example of the kind of spectacle he avoided. "Right
now, though, I just need a favor."

"Sure. Hold on." The phone was muffled for a
moment while she spoke to someone else. Then she
was back. "Whatcha need?"

"Dinner to go for the three of us. I'll pick it up."

"Ooh," she purred. "Romantic."

"Practical," he corrected. "You can save the
chocolate-covered-strawberry theme."

"Taking it slow. Good move." She lost the purr

and sounded typically humorous. "What sort of non-romantic, practical fare do you have in mind?"

Provisions took the farm-to-table concept seriously. "Doesn't matter. She did say to include something that was orange. But not an actual orange."

"Hmm. Not exactly the season for squash," she murmured. "Carrots are easy, of course, but so prosaic."

Were carrots prosaic? He couldn't believe he actually wondered. "Go with those as a last resort."

"That's right. You're the no-carrot boy. Not even carrot cake. I just don't understand that, Stefan. Carrot cake with a thick layer of cream cheese frosting is to *die* for."

So much for keeping the conversation on the rails. "I'll pick it up about a quarter after five."

"What about wine? Red or white?"

"Obviously something from Mendoza Winery," he said automatically.

"Well, duh." She laughed. "I mean do you want me to pair something special with your dinner? Is Justine nursing the baby? Maybe she doesn't drink wine."

She drank wine all right. At least she had seventeen months ago. She also didn't hold it all that well. Now though? Maybe she was nursing the baby. Yet another thing that Stefan didn't know.

That he *should* know.

"Skip the wine."

"Got it. What about dessert?"

"Yeah. Whatever." He knew he sounded impatient. "Just choose whatever you and Rodrigo would want to have after a busy day," he said more calmly. "I trust you."

"Aww. I'm touched, Stefan." She sounded it. "So, a nonromantic, orange-colored comfort meal. We'll have you covered, Stefan. Rosemary's on tonight," she named the head chef, "so you're in good hands. If you want us to run the food out to you, just call when you get here. Otherwise, you can see Tom at the bar. He'll grab it from the kitchen for you."

"Thanks."

"I mean it about setting up a family get-together here at the restaurant," she said before he could hang up. "Be thinking about it, okay?"

He agreed and finally managed to end the call just in time to connect into the video conference with the ad manager at Grayson Gear.

The rest of the afternoon flew by. But the zoning commissioner signed off on the brewery plan quicker than Stefan expected, which meant he had time to grab a shower and shave before he drove into town. It was a Thursday and Provisions was just getting into the early stages of their dinner rush when Stefan went inside to pick up the two large bags of food. He managed to escape without running into Ashley or anyone else.

His truck smelled like roasted chicken and even though he was more accustomed to eating dinner later in the evening, his stomach was growling when he parked at the curb in front of Justine's place.

He pulled out the bags of food and could hear a baby crying before he'd walked halfway up the narrow driveway.

It didn't feel like an auspicious beginning. But even though he had little firsthand experience with babies, he knew enough to know that they cried.

The crying was even louder when he reached the top of the stairs. He doubted there was any chance of Justine hearing his knock.

He tried anyway. She was already as wary of him as Morgan was. Walking in—assuming she didn't have the door locked—was probably the worst thing he could do.

The twine handle of one of the bags was starting to tear away from the paper and he propped the bag on the chair next to the door. From the other side, the baby's crying was reaching an even higher pitch.

His nerves frayed. How would he know if an accident happened?

You can't keep an eye on them 24/7, one part of his head reasoned.

All the more reason to get her to marry you, the other part argued.

He'd planned to gut and remodel the ranch house in one fell swoop. He could make do with living in a single room or two, but if Justine and the baby were there, he should do it in stages. He'd even hire a nanny to help with the baby. He'd already planned to hire a housekeeper.

He knocked again. Harder. "Justine?" He reached for the round doorknob, but the door swung open abruptly.

She stood there, looking perfectly calm in comparison to him.

"What's wrong?" Without waiting for an invitation, he stepped past her, scanning the small living area and galley-style kitchen for signs of calamity. Anything to explain Morgan's high-pitched, hiccupping wails.

But all he saw was the baby corralled safely in a high chair.

His cheeks were red, and he was waving his fists in the air. The floor around him was littered with cereal and toys.

Toys were scattered over the rest of the living area, too.

Books sat stacked on the floor next to one end of the sofa and nearby, an opened laptop sat on a plastic milk crate.

He looked at Justine. The pretty dress from that morning was gone. Instead, she wore denim cutoffs that showed off her long legs and a faded T-shirt that was so loose it showed off nothing at all. Her hair was pulled up in a messy knot on top of her head and she had a pair of gold-rimmed glasses perched on her nose.

Her caramel-brown eyes had been easy to lose

himself in before. Now they looked even larger. Even easier to dive into headlong. "You wear glasses," he said stupidly.

She whipped them off as if she'd forgotten they were there. "So?"

He usually knew the value of silence. He didn't know why he couldn't remember that when he was around her.

Maybe because he tended to forget everything when she was near. Maybe because the glasses had looked sexy as all hell. And he shouldn't be thinking sexy-anything when Morgan was over there screaming his head off. "I didn't know you wore them."

"I didn't." She plucked at a thread on her frayed shorts. "Not then."

Then.

When he'd ignored all his own good sense about staying away from virgins—even ones as appealing as her.

He set the bag on the breakfast counter and retrieved the one from outside.

Meanwhile, Morgan was still wailing, though Stefan could see now that there wasn't a single tear streaming down his son's flushed cheeks.

His son. It was still unsettling.

Unsettling? That was way too mild.

Astonishing? Overwhelming?

Closer. But still not adequate to describe the feelings inside him.

"Temper tantrum?" If his voice sounded a little gruff, he hoped he was the only one who heard it.

Justine nodded. Given her lack of reaction to Morgan's racket, he could only assume that it wasn't an unfamiliar occurrence. "He wants my laptop."

"I'll bring him an old one of mine first thing tomorrow if it keeps him from screaming like that." He offered a half smile.

She didn't return it.

"I was kidding."

He heard her sigh, which was a miracle given the noise coming from one small human.

"Sorry. My sense of humor's gone by the wayside. Obviously." With a determined-looking headshake she peeked inside the first of the two bags. "You really didn't have to bring dinner, but I'd be lying if I said I wasn't happy about it." She gave him a clearly forced smile.

"You look tired."

"Two hours of sleep'll do that." She pulled out one of the containers and popped off the lid. "Grilled melon. Brilliant. When I said something orange, I figured squash or carrots but this—" She lifted a long, slender wedge of cantaloupe with grill marks on its side and took a bite. Her eyes fluttered closed for a moment. "Mmm."

He nearly swallowed his tongue and had to look away. He cleared his throat and shoved his fingers in his pockets. Not even his son's tantrum was enough to distract him from the memory of Justine making that very same sound while they'd made love.

Morgan started slapping his palms against the tray of his high chair. He kicked out a bare foot, but the chair was positioned just far enough away from everything that he didn't connect. A good thing. The base of the chair was obviously designed to prevent tipping from an occupant jerking around the way Morgan was, but if he could push his foot against the wall?

"This orange phase started last week," Justine was saying. "Hopefully it won't last too long." She was thankfully oblivious to Stefan's thoughts as she rounded the breakfast bar and opened a cupboard to pull out a bright green contraption that looked like a shallow bowl molded from a flat square of rubber. "One day, Morgan was eating nearly anything I offered him. Green beans. Bananas. Oatmeal. You name it. Then the next?" She shook her head as she cut the melon into cubes and dropped them into the bowl that she deftly pressed flat onto the high chair tray between Morgan's banging.

Suction, Stefan realized, when the baby immediately tried to shove the bowl aside.

"Ingenious."

"What?" She'd gone back to the bags of food and followed Stefan's attention to Morgan's bowl. "Oh, yeah. Super handy. Kirby introduced me to them. From Kirby's Perks? Have you met her?"

"My contractor just got engaged to her."

She shot him a look. "Your contractor is Josh Fortune?"

He spread his hands. "I didn't choose him just so I could stand here with you glaring at me about it."

She closed her eyes for a moment. "Sorry," she muttered. "This whole situation has—" She broke off. "It doesn't matter. Then you probably know Kirby has two little girls. She's had a lot of helpful hints for me. Like the bowl. I'm hoping to have a few months before he learns how to lift the corners and break the suction."

The baby was more interested in trying to grasp the raised sides of the bowl, which wasn't getting him anywhere. His eyebrows were drawn down in fierce concentration as he yanked. Harder and harder. His crying turned into staccato yelps of temper.

"I don't know if I'm more impressed by his stamina or worried about what it'll mean for the future."

She smiled slightly. It seemed less forced. "He'll give up eventually." She'd finished unloading the bags and folded them flat. "He's just mad and expecting me to respond. When I don't, he'll stop. Besides which, he's used to having food at this hour. And Morgan is nothing if not used to a schedule. Have a seat," she invited abruptly.

He noticed the second bar stool she'd placed on the other side of the counter. It hadn't been there that morning.

She was setting out plates and he straddled the

stool. He would focus on the meal if it killed him. "I hope you like the food. I asked my sister-in-law to—"

Suddenly, the room went silent, except for the sound of Morgan squishing chunks of melon through his fingers.

"—choose everything," he finished.

Justine handed him a napkin. This time the smile was genuine. "Told you."

Morgan lifted his fistful of fruit and smashed it against his mouth. His cheeks were still red, but he was no longer frowning ferociously. In fact, he looked perfectly content.

Stefan was more frazzled than ever.

"Don't worry," Justine said. "He's not Jekyll and Hyde. Just learning his ways of expression."

Better for her to think he was only disturbed by Morgan's fussing. "What about learning the ways of a spoon?"

"He gets more into his mouth this way, plus he's learning dexterity." She held up her hand and pressed her index finger to her thumb. "Pincer grasp. Take it you don't have a lot of encounters with babies his age."

"Shows?"

"I didn't have any experience, either. Pretty much on-the-job training." She dropped more chunks into Morgan's bowl and sat down across from Stefan, only to hop up again. Her cheeks were slightly pink, not unlike Morgan's. "What do you want to drink?

I have iced tea or lemonade. I'd offer milk but I ran out."

"Not much of a milk drinker," he said. The baby—his son—was nearly a carbon copy of Stefan. But he found himself looking at the baby for glimpses of his mother. Not Justine's coloring. That was entirely Stefan's. But the shape of his nose maybe. Or the angle of his chin…

"How about wine?" She'd opened a cupboard door and taken down two wine bottles. "I have red and white. No idea if either is very good. They were gifts from a happy client."

He smiled faintly. He recognized the label. It was good, but not Mendoza Winery good. "Ashley asked if she should include wine with the food. I told her to skip it."

She made a face and returned the bottles to the cupboard. "Considering how well I handled my wine the night we met?" She opened the refrigerator. "Probably smart."

"Actually, Ashley brought up whether or not you were nursing the baby, and I didn't know the answer."

"The pediatrician says that having a glass now and then isn't really harmful for the baby. But, as it happens, I haven't had much wine at all since… since Florida."

"What about Cuban coffee?"

She went still for a moment. "Not since then, either." She sounded husky. She didn't ask him again what his preference was, but simply filled both of their glasses with tea and sat.

His brain had gone from Little Havana to her hotel suite all over again and it was his own damn fault for bringing it up.

She, on the other hand, seemed to be focusing hard on the take-out containers. There was the grilled chicken he'd smelled along with roasted vegetables. She unwrapped a foil-wrapped bundle. "Fish tacos and—" she took a quick taste "—mango salsa." She glanced up at Stefan through her lashes. "Which do you prefer?"

His appetite was growing, and it wasn't for food. "Let's just divide it all up."

They did.

While Morgan chewed on strips of roasted orange bell pepper and Justine slipped in an occasional spoonful of saffron rice, they decimated the tacos and the roast chicken.

"What was the client happy about?" he asked when they were finally winding down and debating whether they had room for the wedge of chocolate torte that Ashley had included.

Justine lifted her gaze to him. "Client?" The lasciviousness in her eyes for the dessert hadn't quite cleared away.

Stefan's self-control was still tenuous and he quickly focused on Morgan. The baby had orange food in his hair, on his face, his arms, his hands and it was painted across the high chair. He was a mess, but he was happy, babbling away and banging the spoon he'd finally wrested away from his mommy.

Stefan chanced a glance back at Justine, only to catch her dipping the tines of her fork through the pointed end of the torte. He exhaled carefully and focused on the baby again. "The one who gave you the wine?" he prompted.

"Her name's Lillian Chavez. She does virtual singing telegrams if you're ever in the market for such a thing. And before you ask, she'd rather I spread the word about her than keep her name confidential like some of my other clients. I handle her bookkeeping. She sent the wine last Christmas."

"You're a bookkeeper?"

"Virtual assistant. I do all sorts of things." She set down her fork with finality. She'd neatly amputated the very tip of the chocolate torte.

"Some days it seems like everything is turning virtual."

"It's meant I can work without having to put Morgan in childcare so you won't hear me complaining." She deftly separated the tray from the high chair and lifted the baby out of it. "And it is time for your bath, isn't it, Master Maloney?"

"Mendoza," Stefan said abruptly. "His name should be Mendoza."

So much for letting Justine set the pace.

Chapter Five

His name should be Mendoza.

Stefan's words hung in the air. Justine looked at him, but she was also hearing her mother's shrill voice when Justine had admitted she was pregnant.

What do you mean, there's no father?

Kimberly had been beside herself when she'd followed Justine through the house. As if waving that "plus-for-positive" test stick that she'd snatched right out of Justine's hand was somehow going to make Justine take back the truth.

That she *was* going to have a baby.

On her own.

No prospective father around, much less a man

to save her from disgrace by putting a wedding ring on her finger.

You don't know how hard you'll have it, Justine! Trying to raise a baby on your own? Everyone in this town is going to talk. Don't you care about this family's reputation at all?

Morgan's wet, open-mouthed kiss on her cheek did what her willpower couldn't—sent the memories back into a box and slammed down the lid.

She stepped around Stefan. "We can talk about it after his bath."

Stefan followed her into the bedroom and for once she was glad for the lifelong habit that Kimberly had drilled into her of making up her bed every day. The space was so small it would have felt crowded with only her narrow bed and chest of drawers. Add to it a crib, rocking chair and changing table, and a person barely had room to turn around. But at least she didn't have her tousled comforter and pillows strewn about as well.

She stopped long enough to pull out a clean sleeper from a drawer and left it on the changing table before going into the bathroom that was as miniature in scale as the rest of the apartment.

She started the faucet running in the shallow bathtub and squirted a measure of baby soap into the stream of water. She stripped off Morgan's clothes and the diaper beneath. Trying to ignore Stefan's presence was pointless. His wide shoulders prac-

tically filled the entire doorway to the bathroom.
"Would you mind getting a clean washcloth from
under the sink?" She could have reached it herself,
but she would have brushed against him no matter
how careful she tried to be.

The bathroom was just that small.

He opened the drawer and handed her a small blue
cloth from inside.

She knelt next to the tub and swished the thin
layer of bubbles around while she waited for the
water to warm up just a little more.

"What about a towel?" Stefan asked.

She felt her cheeks flush. If it wasn't for him, she
wouldn't have to concentrate so hard on things that
were second nature by now. The metal towel rack
affixed to the white wall was lamentably bare. Had
this been a normal evening, she'd have noticed that
before she'd even started the water running. "They're
still in the dryer," she admitted.

"Just tell me that doesn't involve a four-block
drive to a laundromat."

She smiled despite herself. "In the garage downstairs. I share the washer and dryer with my landlady.
Key is hanging on the peg next to the refrigerator."

He nodded and took his wide shoulders and the
rest of his disturbing self out of the doorway. A moment later, she heard his footsteps on the staircase.

She pulled in a long, deep breath and turned off
the faucet. Morgan was squirming in her arms, trying to climb into the tub, and she checked the tem-

perature one more time before lowering him into the water.

He laughed and sat right down, immediately smacking his palms waterward and sending up a big splash.

"Come on, bug," she murmured, trying to distract him with one of his bath toys. "Can we leave some water in the tub for once?"

The answer to that was a typical and vehement no.

By the time Stefan returned with the towels, Justine's T-shirt was wet all down the front. Despite that, she'd washed Morgan clean in nearly record time and she lifted him out of the water and wrapped him in the towel that Stefan handed her.

He backed out of the doorway, and she carried Morgan to the changing table. "You can drop the rest of the towels anywhere."

He chose the foot of her bed. But he didn't just leave them in a pile.

He proceeded to fold them.

She was pretty sure she'd never seen anyone of the male persuasion fold towels. Not even her brothers.

Stefan must have noticed her surprise. "What?"

She shook her head slightly. "Nothing."

She was used to the nightly tussle that ensued after Morgan's bath and managed to get him into a fresh diaper even though he flipped over onto his hands and knees midway through. He wasn't having the stretchy sleeper at all though. No way. No how.

She gave up and settled for one of his soft white

T-shirts that she kept in a stack on the shelf beneath the changing table.

"Looks like that shirt barely fits," Stefan said.

She tried not to bristle as she scooped Morgan up in her arms again. "He's a growing baby. Every two weeks he grows out of something."

"I just meant—" He sighed and turned back to the neat stack of towels. "Where do these go?"

"Two on the towel rack. The rest under the sink." She plucked at the front of her wet shirt as she carried Morgan back into the living area. She'd need to nurse him soon.

She started to set him on the floor so she could clean up from dinner, but he fussed and clung to her neck like a limpet, dragging at her shirt. She gave him his blankie from the floor and bounced him around, hoping that her milk didn't let down just yet. She carried him into the kitchen and began transferring the empty take-out containers to the trash can with her free hand.

"I'll do that," Stefan offered. "I might as well be useful," he added when she started to shake her head.

Morgan was fussing even more.

"Fine. I need to feed him, anyway." She saw Stefan's skeptical glance toward the high chair that still needed to be wiped clean. "Breastfeed him," she elaborated and returned to the bedroom, before closing the door.

Morgan wasted no time the second she settled in the rocking chair. She closed her eyes, humming softly. But the usual peacefulness of nursing him eluded her.

Fortunately, Morgan didn't notice.

After he was finished, she changed his diaper and her own shirt and went back into the living area.

It was neat as a pin. High chair cleaned and tucked back in the corner out of the way. The breakfast bar was cleared, and all the toys had been picked up from the floor and placed in the plastic milk crate. Even the ones from under the couch where Stefan was sitting.

"Abnormal psychology." He was paging through her textbook. "Some heavy stuff in there."

"Social work can be a heavy field." Drowsy and blissed out on milk, Morgan was at his most snuggly. "Do you want to try holding him?" She didn't wait for the answer that she knew anyway and leaned over to settle Morgan in his arms.

But midtransfer, huge tears welled in Morgan's eyes. "Mamaaaaaaaa." He twisted Justine's blouse in one fist, keeping her bent awkwardly over them both.

"Tears are the killer," Stefan muttered, lifting the baby back toward her again.

Their hands brushed and as soon as she'd straightened again, he pushed off the couch as if a spring had been poking him in the rear.

"He'll get used to you in time," she said.

"Time would go a lot faster if you—"

"Don't start. I'm not marrying you."

He didn't lose a beat. "Then move in with me." He

snatched up the small stack of bills on her counter. "You wouldn't have to worry about past-due notices for your electricity."

She gaped. "You went through my *mail*?"

He dropped the envelopes again. "What's to go through? They're sitting right here in the open. If you don't want them to be seen, put them away."

"Next time I will." Cradling the baby, she swayed back and forth, soothing him but not really soothing herself. She'd shove the bills in the same drawer where the credit card he'd pressed on her had been shoved.

Regardless of where she kept her bills though, the damage was already done. He'd seen enough. And now he'd have that ammunition at his disposal, too.

The mother of the infant in question is unable to maintain a proper home environment...

How many reports had she written up containing those very words when she'd been interning in Houston while earning her undergraduate degree?

She watched Stefan pace from one corner of her apartment to the other. It reminded her of a big cat pacing in a cage.

"It's a decent-sized house," he said. "I'm planning renovations to modernize it. But there are already plenty of bedrooms. Morgan could have his own." He reached the corner and pivoted on his heel again. His green gaze collided with hers. "You, too. It goes without saying. Obviously. You'll have your space. I'll have mine."

He couldn't have made it plainer that he wasn't interested in those spaces...mingling.

"We're fine here," she insisted.

He looked like he wanted to argue. But he didn't. "Keep an open mind. There's no danger in that."

There was every danger.

She'd spent less than twenty-four hours with him a year and a half ago and still relived every minute during her dreams. How on earth would she manage when—*if*—they were living beneath the same roof?

He wasn't pursuing *her*. He was pursuing Morgan.

She just happened to come along with the package.

She pressed her lips against Morgan's head. The soft curls in his glossy brown hair were springing up as they dried. His father's hair had done exactly the same thing after the one shower they'd shared.

Even now her fingertips tingled with the sensation of twining through Stefan's hair. "I need to put him down for the night," she said abruptly.

Stefan stopped pacing. He lifted his hand and rubbed the back of his neck. "You said you usually go to the park every day."

"Usually."

"I'll see you there tomorrow, then."

She couldn't help it. "Unless something more important comes up again."

His lips thinned. "Have you ever worried about Morgan's health?"

"What? No. Thankfully." She shifted the baby in

her arms. He was already starting to doze off. "I told you. He's had the best of care at the pediatric center."

"He's perfectly healthy," he pressed.

"Perfectly. What are you trying to suggest?"

"You—*we*—have a healthy baby. Not every parent is as lucky. And my business partner happens to be one of them. A couple years ago, Adam and Laurel weren't even sure their baby would live. So, yeah. When he told me Larkin has a fever and they've gotta take him to Houston, I told him not to worry about anything else. Even though that meant I wasn't going to be able to get to the park this afternoon."

She felt lower than a worm in the mud.

She *had* been blessed with a healthy baby. She'd even had an easy pregnancy—at least health-wise— once her initial morning sickness had waned. "If… if something comes up tomorrow, maybe we could meet you another time. Or I could bring him to see you. Somewhere." She swallowed past the tightness in her throat. "I do most of my studying and work when Morgan's sleeping anyway so if we need to be flexible when he's not…" She lifted her shoulders. She couldn't tell at all what Stefan was thinking. She just knew that she felt nervous when he watched her like he was watching her now.

"You work when he sleeps," he said. "And study when he sleeps."

"It's not unheard of."

He pinched the bridge of his nose. "No wonder you haven't been able to finish your master's degree yet," he muttered. He dropped his hand and opened the door. "I'll call you tomorrow. We'll play it by ear. See how the day goes."

She nodded. She liked routine and order and schedules. But she also didn't want to be as rabid about it as her mother had always been. She didn't want Morgan to grow up and leave one day like her brothers had because she was too rigidly set in her ways to adjust if or when she needed to adjust. "Thanks again for bringing dinner. And—" she jerked her chin, encompassing the living area "—picking up, to boot."

"You're not in this alone, Justine."

Her throat tightened up all over again. Whatever she said would be a croak so she just nodded and pressed her cheek against Morgan's sweet-smelling curls.

"Move in with me and I can hire some help. A nanny."

The warmth froze in place. Her "I don't need a nanny" came out crystal clear.

"Even if it would mean having more than an hour or two a day to study?"

She stared back at him silently.

He sighed again and stepped through the doorway. "I'll call you tomorrow."

She didn't stand there to watch him go down the stairs. She pushed the door closed and flipped the lock.

She'd hung a narrow decorative mirror near the door, and in the reflection, she could see Morgan's eyes were closed. His lashes were long dark crescents against his cheeks. His lips were slightly parted, almost like he was starting to smile.

"Nanny," she whispered under her breath. "As if."

She held Morgan close for a long, long while before she carried him into the bedroom and laid him in his crib.

"And then what happened?"

Justine leaned her head back against the lawn chair outside her front door while Garland's question circled in her mind. "I took Morgan out of his high chair and went to start his bath."

"I mean with *Stefan*," Garland prompted. "What happened after he said you and Morgan should move in with him?"

"I said no. Of course." Just as she'd done when he'd proposed marriage.

"Why?"

She pulled her feet down from where she'd propped them on the wood railing. "I don't even *know* him!" Her voice rose and somewhere nearby a dog barked.

"Except in the biblical sense," Garland countered.

"And I really don't even know why I'm telling you about it," she added, lowering her voice again.

"Well, *thanks*."

Justine leaned over and picked up the bottle of wine that she'd opened.

Stefan had left hours ago. Morgan hadn't stirred.

Anyone who drinks alone is on the road to ruin.

She deliberately poured several inches of red wine on top of the first inch in the juice glass and mentally saluted one of her mother's favorite refrains.

"You know what I mean, Garland. He doesn't really mean it. It's not like *he* intends to help with diaper changes and entertaining an infant."

"I don't know. Stefan didn't strike me as a guy who'd give up very easily. He didn't when it came to that business deal with Victor."

"What *was* that deal, anyway? Did we ever really know?"

"Not you with your nose in a textbook, apparently. He signed Victor to a distribution deal for the winery."

"What winery?"

"Mendoza Winery. What do you think?"

She nearly choked on her sip of wine. "He has a *winery*? He never told me that!"

"Too busy with the crazy mad sex." Garland's voice was full of laughter. "I think it's a family thing or something. I remember seeing a commercial last year when I was in Houston for Christmas. Hold on. I'm looking it—yep. The Mendoza Winery. Founded by…ah, let's see. Alejandro Mendoza and cousins. Man, those Mendoza men are *hot*. There are headshots of them all on the website. Then a bunch of awards for their wines, yada yada. A bunch of links to restaurants, too. La Viña at the winery. *Gorgeous* venue. I bet they could host some amazing events."

Justine could hear Garland tapping on her keyboard through the phone.

"Interesting. They must be connected to Red. The restaurant in Red Rock. Have you heard of it? The place is famous. That country singer who turned up after weeks of being missing and had the concert in Rambling Rose last year? Jett Carr? Says here he's shooting a music video there soon."

Justine knew from experience that her friend had gone down the rabbit hole of internet links again. "I'll have to take your word for it." She sipped her wine even though it made her mouth pucker and wondered why Stefan hadn't said a word about the winery when they'd been talking about wine. "When are you heading back to Chicago?"

"Not for another few weeks and six, count 'em, six events."

"Your schedule sounds exhausting."

"Talking to me at two in the morning while you're between posting drivel on the webbernet for other people and writing term papers while your baby sleeps sounds exhausting. Will you change his last name to Mendoza?"

"I haven't thought that far. I'm just trying to get through the next day."

"Would it be so bad, Jus? Moving in with him?"

"Yes!"

"Why? It did take the two of you to create Morgan. Let him help with the work that resulted."

"*He's* not going to help. He said he'd hire a nanny."

"And your point is?"

"I see your maternal instincts are as deep as ever."

"Should have thought twice about making me his godmother, then."

"Yes, well, I figured by asking both you and Debbie, you'd balance out each other." If Anika hadn't died, the three of them would have been Morgan's godmothers.

Practically a fairy tale.

"Just keep an open mind," Garland urged. "About moving in. It doesn't mean you have to agree to a nanny."

"I'm not trying to be close-minded. I just don't want to make another—" She stopped herself. Not *another* mistake. She was never going to consider Morgan's existence to be a mistake. "The only reason I have such a good deal on rent is because Gwen is Debbie's aunt. If I move in with him, Gwen will have no problem renting this place out. I can't expect her to keep it vacant for me when things fail. And then where does that leave me? Tucking my tail and going back to my mother?" The idea made her mouth pucker worse than the wine.

"Maybe they won't fail."

"Has spending so much time in Japan unearthed a vein of optimism in you?"

"Not likely. But you *are* an optimistic soul, Justine. You always have been. You're the best of us all."

Justine shook her head. "Anika was the best of

us all." Then her eyes stung. That's what she got for having even a few sips of wine. She descended right into maudlin sentimentality.

"I figure heaven needed some help," Garland said after a moment. The sound of her computer keys had stopped. "It's the only reason she got taken from us slobs down here. *But*, on that optimistic note, that means she's up there waving her wings. You've got to admit, it's oddly coincidental for you and Stefan to *both* land in Rambling Rose."

"Or the universe is just having a laugh at our expense."

"Come on," Garland chided. "Wouldn't you rather think it's Anika sprinkling some magic?"

"Or mischief."

"Mischief's my domain. There's a reason you were in that coffee shop the other day. A reason why Stefan stopped in there."

"Yes, and her name is Bonita," Justine said darkly. Which was silly. She couldn't be jealous. She'd had a one-night stand with Stefan. Not a relationship.

"But Stefan's not asking Bonita to move in with him." Garland's voice turned serious. "He's asking *you*, Justine, and if there is a mistake in there, it's you not giving it at least some real consideration. You're supposed to be the most reasoned one of us all. Remember?"

Justine sighed. "I don't think I've felt *reasoned* since Stefan and I met."

"You'll do the right thing," Garland said. "You always do."

Justine appreciated her friend's faith.

She just wasn't sure she deserved it.

Chapter Six

Garland's words remained stuck in Justine's mind the next afternoon as she followed the directions Stefan had texted to her.

"We're just driving out to his house because it's easier for us to go to *him* today." She looked in her rearview mirror to the car seat positioned behind her. "It doesn't mean I'm changing my mind about us living with your daddy."

Morgan continued chewing on the rubbery head of his skinny giraffe toy, not a care in the world.

It was her job to keep him that secure for as long as she could.

She focused on the road.

It was narrow. Graded but not paved. And it

snaked through the low rolling grassland with no end in sight.

Stefan had said the property was several miles outside town and she was certain that she'd turned off the highway at the correct spot. But right now, it felt like she was driving out to the middle of nowhere.

She glanced at the cardboard box on the passenger seat beside her. When she'd passed Mariana's Market on their way out of town, she'd impetuously stopped. With Morgan strapped in the carrier, she'd walked through the flea market, teeming with shoppers especially on a Friday, to the center where Mariana's food truck was always positioned. She'd bought a couple of sandwiches, a couple of iced teas and a strawberry tart.

It wasn't much, but it made her feel like she was restoring just a little balance to the seesaw she'd been strapped to since encountering Stefan in Kirby's Perks.

Morgan was singing gleefully to his giraffe. Tunelessly. Nonsensically.

Listening to him was better than any song on the radio. Which was good since hers had gone out and she couldn't afford to fix it.

The road curved around a tree, with such enormous branches they reached nearly to the ground again, before cresting a small rise.

When she reached the top, she saw the house.

White house, he'd said. *You won't miss it.*

What she saw seemed so much more.

Black shutters bracketed the windows that marched evenly across the front of the white house. Both stories of it. Thick patches of pink-and-yellow flowers grew on both sides of the three steps that led up to the wide covered porch that spanned the length of the house.

It was the kind of house that looked as if it had stood there for generations. And would keep standing for generations more.

Her palms felt sweaty as she slowed and turned onto the gravel drive ending in a half circle in front of the house.

Up close, she could see that the white paint needed a good refresher. That the black shutters really weren't as glossy as they'd first seemed.

She didn't want to, but she loved the house anyway.

She was unbuckling Morgan from the car seat when the front door opened, and Stefan appeared. He was wearing khaki cargo shorts and an ivory T-shirt that clung to his chest.

"Need help?"

She started to shake her head but made herself stop. "There's a box in the front seat." She lifted Morgan out before grabbing her backpack and pushing the door closed with her hip just in time for Stefan to reach the car.

"What's in the box?" He opened the passenger door.

"Call it late lunch? Early dinner?" It was after three in the afternoon. "Nothing anywhere near as fancy as dinner last night. Just a couple sandwiches from Mariana's food truck at the flea market. If you haven't been there yet, you're missing out." If she kept talking, she could keep from dwelling on how good he smelled. His hair was combed back from his face, looking slightly damp.

It took no imagination at all to realize he'd showered.

Recently.

"I know Mariana but not from the market. I stayed at Hotel Fortune when I first moved here. She's one of the chefs at the restaurant there. Roja. Been there?"

The food truck was kinder to her budget. The cost of one restaurant meal meant a week of coffees at Kirby's Perks.

She didn't say that though. She just shook her head and took a few steps away from the car. "How'd you even find this place?" she asked. "It's definitely off the beaten track and in Miami you—" Did she really want to bring up Miami?

Of course, it was too late. Stefan was giving her a curious look. "In Miami, I…?"

"Didn't strike me as a countryside farmhouse type of guy."

He raised an eyebrow. "What did I strike you as?"

She should have kept her mouth shut. "Insanely popular Miami nightclubs. Modern art and high-rise apartments."

His teeth flashed. "Pretty spot-on. But as it happens, it surprises me, too." He tucked the box under his arm and slid the backpack off her arm as well. "Come on inside. It's hot out here."

It was hot.

Looking at Stefan was what made her feel like melting though.

She focused on the flowers rather than the back view of him as she followed him toward the house. They were lush, but too scraggly. Nothing that a little pinching back wouldn't solve.

Morgan batted her in the face with his giraffe.

Yeah, that's right. Get your head where it belongs, Mommy.

They went up the stairs. The wood porch needed a good sanding and refinishing. And a couple of rocking chairs. There was certainly room enough for several.

"I'm thinking about ordering a porch swing," he said as he pushed open the front door and stepped back for her to enter. "What do you think?"

"Good idea." Bemused and unnerved, she held her breath as she passed him. If she didn't breathe, then she couldn't inhale the scent of him, right?

Wrong.

Despite the numerous windows, the interior was decidedly dim after the bright sunshine. She could still see the boxes stacked against the walls in the otherwise empty room.

"Come on to the family room," he said. "Not as depressing as the parlor there."

Parlor. It fit that an old farmhouse would possess such a thing.

The wood floor creaked slightly as she followed him down a cave-like hallway and through the doorway of the kitchen.

The appliances were ugly but her entire apartment could have fit in the space.

The family room was off the kitchen and was obvious, if only because a wooden sign on the wall said Family Room in large looping letters. There was also a big couch upholstered in scarred brown leather and wood trunk in place of a coffee table.

"You hungry right now or would you rather have the full tour?" Stefan set the backpack on the couch and the box on the trunk and began unloading it.

His hair was starting to curl at the nape of his neck. It would twirl around her fingertip the same way Morgan's did.

She looked away and hitched Morgan higher on her hip before picking up one of the iced teas. "The full tour but only if you agree not to make something more out of it." She deftly flipped the tab on the cup lid with her thumb and took a sip.

He straightened. "I'll try to control myself." He took the other drink. "Does the tart need to go in the fridge?"

"I'm sure it'll be fine for a while." She'd already told herself they would stay for no more than an hour. She could handle anything for an hour.

She hoped.

She followed him back into the kitchen. "Did you have a lot of houses to choose from when you started looking?"

"Not many. The nine acres it sits on were more of a priority than the house. They border Adam's place." He must have read her blank expression as easily as he'd read her mind about the porch. "Adam Fortune. My business partner."

"I thought you were partners with your brothers. Mendoza Winery?" She'd spent Morgan's morning naptime scouring the webbernet as Garland called it, reading everything she could find about the family Mendoza. "Why didn't you mention you had your own winery last night?"

Morgan chattered nonsensically and threw his giraffe almost at Stefan's head.

He caught it before it hit. "I thought you knew." He held the giraffe out toward Morgan.

The baby ignored the toy and pressed his face resolutely against Justine's neck.

Stefan's gaze shifted to her face. "Does it really matter?"

"It does if you think being rich matters where Morgan is concerned." No doubt *he'd* never been late with an electric bill in his life.

"I guess if I'm ever rich, I'll put some thought into it."

She set her tea on the scarred counter and snatched the giraffe from his fingers. "You own a winery, *and* you just bought this place. That you've already told me you'll be renovating." He even had a stack of architectural drawings that she could see sitting on the kitchen table. "You're saying you don't have money?"

"I have enough to be comfortable. And to make things easier for you."

Comfortable was clearly a subjective term.

"I told you a house tour didn't mean—"

He raised his palm. "Just a general statement of fact, Justine. Don't read more into it than it is. So. Kitchen. The footprint is okay as is but all the rest has to change." He turned away from her and pulled open a lower cabinet that was really a hinged bin. "Of course, these old cupboards—"

"Are wonderful," she said before she could help herself.

His eyebrows went up slightly as he looked her way.

One of the advantages of carrying around a baby all the time was that she could focus on him whenever it was convenient. Like when she had no self-control over her tongue. "Quintessential farmhouse." She was proud of the blithe tone. She wished she felt as blithe about the reality of his apparent financial resources in comparison to her own.

"We'll see," he said, thankfully oblivious to her thoughts. He closed the bin again and led the way out of the kitchen.

In addition to the rooms she'd already seen, the main floor possessed a large study and a laundry room that put the stacked washer and dryer in

Gwen's garage to shame. The staircase, when they got to it, was more utilitarian than showpiece. Going up on one side to the upper floor, and on the other down to the basement that Stefan said wasn't worth seeing. "Light's bad anyway," he said and offered again to carry the baby.

And once again Morgan refused to cooperate.

"How much does he weigh?"

"Twenty-two pounds. And he was twenty-eight inches at his last checkup." She started up the stairs. "I'm used to carrying him. I just didn't think to bring in the carrier from the car. Strap him on and we're both good to go for hours. Oh. I should have asked." She stopped midstep and looked back.

Stefan nearly bumped into her. "Need to put some brake lights on you." He took a step down, which left them at eye level.

He was still so close she could see the faint flecks of gold in his eyes that made the green that much greener. She lowered her gaze, but that just meant she was looking at his mouth. Her heart skittered around and she backed up to the next stair tread. "I meant to ask you earlier how Larkin was doing."

"He's better." Stefan advanced another stair. "Fever's gone. They were heading back from Houston this morning."

She hadn't noticed where he'd left his cup of iced tea along the way. But his hands were empty now and clasped around the railings attached to the wall on either side of them. He looked imposing and way too sexy.

She switched Morgan to her other side and continued up the staircase.

"They must be very relieved," she managed. "What does Adam do at the winery?"

"Nothing. He's been at Provisions as an assistant manager and brewing beer on the side. But now we're partners in building an actual brewery. He'll brew. I'll market. The plans are in the kitchen. I'll show them to you when we go back downstairs."

She reached the landing and glanced back at him. "What comes next after the brewery? A distillery?"

He flashed a smile and a fresh generation of butterflies burst to life inside her.

"Beer and wine are it for now. Someone else can handle the hard stuff." He took another step, cutting the gap between them in half.

The fluttering grew frenzied. For an insane moment she thought he was going to kiss her. But all he did was move around her to take the tour-guide lead again.

She pressed her head against Morgan's and exhaled.

"All the bedrooms are up here," he said. The worn wooden floor creaked comfortably every other step. The plaster walls needed fresh paint, but the ceilings were high and the hallway was wide. "Not to suggest anything—" he turned a crystal-like doorknob and pushed open a door "—but this bathroom could be pretty comfortable." He waited a beat. "If someone was looking for such a thing."

The sight of the deep claw-foot tub sitting below a wide-mullioned window was enough to make her heart clutch. Just a little. The floor, though, was a mess of glue-down squares that were cracked and lifting at the corners. "What's that?" She pointed to a flat panel—about two feet square—cut into the wall next to the pedestal sink that had a faded blue chintz skirt around it.

"Laundry chute." He pushed the panel and it swung inward from its hinge at the top. "Laundry room is directly below."

"Too bad there's not a dumbwaiter to bring it back up again all folded and ready to put away."

"That's one of the things I pay my housekeeper to do."

Housekeeper.

Just keep on walking, Justine.

She did, but admittedly, her gaze lingered on the bathroom. Having a housekeeper scrub the bathtubs was a lot more appealing than she wanted to admit.

He showed her the rest of the bedrooms. Four in all. One next to the bathroom. Two across from it. All three of them were easily twice the size of the bedroom at her apartment, though she noticed the closets were miniscule. The kind of closets that meant using chifforobes and armoires.

She didn't speculate about the bedroom at the end of the hall. It was obviously Stefan's master suite.

And it was the only one that had a bed in it.

She glimpsed the foot of it—and the bedding that was trailing off the end—and immediately looked away.

The damage was done though. Her mind was busy conjuring visions of his long, lean body draped only in a white sheet.

"I need to change Morgan." She escaped back down the hallway, the floor squeaking loudly. He'd said he was going to have the floor redone, and everything else modernized.

Except for the bathroom floor, she disagreed on all fronts.

She surreptitiously eyed the claw-foot tub as she passed it again, only to bounce her shoulder off the doorjamb when she walked right into it.

"Okay there?" he asked behind her.

She was flushing. "Yes." She quickly skipped down the staircase and returned to the family room.

She grabbed a fresh diaper and wipes from the backpack and deftly flipped out the changing pad on the floor next to the coffee-table trunk. Then she laid Morgan back on it. As soon as she freed him from the soaked diaper, he was ready to roam.

"Oh no you don't, mister," she warned, holding her hand on his chest while she washed him with a baby wipe. "Play time hits new heights when he gets his diaper off." Only around Stefan did her nerves make her chatter so much. She let go of Morgan long enough to wrap the wipe inside the wet diaper and fasten it into a ball with the tapes.

It was all the opportunity the baby needed. He flipped onto his belly and started scooting across the oval braided rug, not bothered in the slightest by the loose romper flapping around his bare little butt.

Stefan's lips tilted slightly. "Can't say I blame him, but…" He scooped up the baby before he got more than a few feet.

Morgan looked startled.

And peed on the front of Stefan's shirt.

"Oh, geez!" She launched off her knees to take the baby and shoved the hem of her own T-shirt in front of the stream. But the worst was already done. "I should've warned you."

"Baptized by pee." Stefan was laughing as he peeled his shirt over his head. "Definitely a first."

She'd carried the memory of Stefan in her mind for a year and a half. But it was nothing compared to the real thing standing two feet away from her, wiping his bundled T-shirt over his abdomen.

What did he need a brewery for when he possessed a six-pack like that?

She focused hard on Morgan as she wrangled him back onto the changing pad and blindly extended the pack of wipes toward Stefan.

And froze when her knuckles brushed warm, bare skin.

He'd crouched next to her.

She stared at him. Not even able to produce a "sorry." Her mouth ran dry.

His fingers brushed hers as he took the wipes, but he didn't open it. When he leaned even closer, her stomach did a slow somersault. If he kissed her, she was a goner. She knew it, but she couldn't make herself move away. His thick lashes lowered slightly and his lips curved.

She swallowed and moistened her lips, leaning in to meet him halfway—

He kept leaning, going right beyond her altogether as he reached around her to catch Morgan who was busy crawling away again.

Her cheeks burned. She sat back on her heels and snatched up the diaper she'd dropped.

"Do you have a spare shirt for yourself?"

A reminder that—while he was all gorgeously bare-chested, she just had a big wet spot on the front of her T-shirt.

"Should be one in the backpack." She slid Morgan away from Stefan who moved to sit on the couch while he looked through the backpack.

Of *course* he hadn't been going to kiss her. He was all about platonic marriage proposals and separate bedrooms…

She fastened Morgan into the diaper and began snapping together his romper.

"I don't see a spare shirt in here." Stefan had emptied the entire contents of the backpack onto the couch.

Several toys. A faded receiving blanket patterned in red trucks. Extra baby wipes. Extra diapers. Extra clothes, extra baby food. Leak pads for her bra that she'd forgotten were even in there, two paper-wrapped tampons and a dog-eared paperback.

He held up the book. *Ten Thousand and One Popular Baby Names*. "Is this where you came up with Morgan's name?"

She wished he would show more attention to his own shirt—or lack of one. "You know where I got the name," she said a little waspishly.

He flipped through the pages anyway. "This thing was published twenty-five years ago."

"It belonged to my mother." Justine had kept it, mostly because she'd seen the names her mother had circled in it. Five names. All boys.

He flipped some more pages. "H, I, J." He stopped flipping. "Julie. June. Justine. 'Meaning—a feminine form of Justin.' Imaginative." He tossed the book into the backpack.

"Yeah, well, if I'd come into the world in a masculine form, maybe my father would have stuck around." Instead, she'd been born a girl. The book had gotten shoved onto a bookshelf by her mother and forgotten until Justine came across it a year ago when she'd been boxing up the books so she could use the shelving for baby supplies.

She finished the last snap and grabbed the receiving blanket. She spread it out and set Morgan on it along with his toys, though there was little chance of him actually remaining on the thin, flannel square.

Stefan was looking at her as if he was trying to figure something out. "Why *did* you name him after the restaurant?"

"I liked the name." She had four brothers, she reminded herself. Stefan was hardly the only man she'd ever seen shirtless.

He was just the only one she'd ever slept with.

She started loading the items into the backpack in an orderly way. One of the tampons had rolled to the edge of the couch right next to his thigh.

You'll do the right thing.

She looked at Morgan, chewing the giraffe's head at the same time as his fist. "I named him Morgan because being at Morgan's with you was a very good memory," she admitted huskily. "Even after the shock of realizing I was pregnant." She didn't dare look at Stefan. If she did, the prickling in her eyes might get even more out of hand. "We ended up with something extraordinary." She stacked several diapers together with precision and despite her intention, flicked a glance his way.

Instead of getting hung up over the wealth of bronzed skin her eyes collided with his.

She blinked hard.

"I *am* sorry that I didn't try to contact you. Even before I lost the connection through Anika and Victor. Then after they died—" Her voice cracked and he suddenly reached out and cupped her cheek.

She closed her eyes and savored the touch.

It was much, much too brief.

The couch creaked as he got up and left the room.

She wiped her nose and pushed to her feet. Morgan had already crawled halfway across the room. She moved him back to his toys and sat down beside him.

Stefan returned. He'd put on a clean gray shirt and held out another to her.

She took it.

"I tried looking you up in Austin." She fingered the folded shirt. "Do you know how many Mendozas there are listed? If I'd have known about the winery—"

He sat on the wooden trunk. "I was talking to Victor *about* the winery when we met."

"When we met, I wasn't interested in what you and Victor were talking about. I was just interested in—" She cleared her throat. "Well, you know."

"Sex." He suddenly looked amused. Whether that was because of her apparent inability to voice the obvious or because that's how he remembered her was up for grabs.

There was no point telling him it hadn't been just sex with anyone. But sex with *him*. Gorgeous, sexy Stefan. Whom she'd never expected to see again after that fantasy-like weekend.

"If I had known that you were the owner of Mendoza Winery—"

"I'm not *the* owner. I own a share like all my brothers."

Splitting hairs, she thought. "If I had known," she repeated doggedly, "I'd like to say that I'd have told you about Morgan. Just because it was the right thing to do." She shrugged. "But I don't want to lie now and say for sure that I would have because I... I just don't know." She forced a smile. She was well aware that she'd pursued him in Miami. Not the other way around. Even more aware that he'd tried avoiding the chase altogether when she'd told him she was a virgin.

"Whether you want to hear it or not, though, I *do* know that I've never held you responsible for my decisions." Something her mother had never understood at all.

He sighed. "It took two of us, Justine."

"Well." Her throat ached. She finished filling the backpack but kept out one of the pouches of baby food. The house tour had taken longer than she'd anticipated and Morgan needed a snack. "Anyway, I am sorry. It doesn't make up for—"

"It's done." His voice was calm. As calm as it had been the night they'd met when he'd held back her hair while she puked up wine and crème brûlée. "Let's just deal with what happens from this point forward. Can we agree on that at least?"

She nodded. "Yes."

"Good. Now go on and change."

"Might as well wait." She showed him the front

of the pouch. "Avocado, carrot and coconut cream. If it's not suitably orange enough, I'll likely end up wearing it anyway."

"When it comes to carrots, I'll be the last one to blame him for spitting them out. Don't you need a spoon or something?"

She wasn't sure where her it came from, but she couldn't stop the sudden smile on her face. "Watch and learn." She twisted off the cap and Morgan snatched the pouch and sucked on the spout.

Justine held her breath. For a lingering, fingers-crossed moment, she'd thought he was satisfied. That he'd swallowed the mouthful of food.

Until his nose scrunched up and his eyebrows drew down almost comically and he spit it all right back out at her. He shook his head, still wearing that fierce look of displeasure and squirmed away from her to chew on his giraffe.

She looked at Stefan who—to his credit—was doing his best not to laugh while he held a baby wipe out to her.

"At least we didn't get any on the floor." She re-capped the pouch and wiped up her shirt.

In eight months, she'd gotten used to spit-up, pee spouts and explosive diapers. A mouthful of mildly chunky green foodstuff was child's play.

"What kind were the other pouches?"

"One is blueberries and spinach. The other one is chicken and beets. I know. Not good planning on my part." She blamed Stefan for that. Or to be more accurate, she blamed her inability to think straight where he was concerned.

"Sounds disgusting. Who comes up with those combinations?"

"Baby food experts. You would be amazed at the choices. I started out making my own food for him, but I was throwing out as much as I was keeping because he really doesn't eat that much solid food yet. I usually try to keep cooked carrots ready. He loves those." She tickled Morgan's belly. "Don't you, bug?" He squeaked with laughter and climbed over her so he was propped up on one knee and one foot. He only wobbled a little.

At the rate he was going, she wondered if he'd progress straight from scooting to walking.

She glanced at Stefan. "What I'd like to know is how can he *know* the stuff in the pouch wasn't orange when it went straight into his mouth?"

"He's brilliant," Stefan said matter-of-factly. Then he gave her a quick wink. "Must take after you."

Chapter Seven

Justine was still wearing Stefan's Dolphins T-shirt
when she left a few hours later. It was faded and too
big, reaching past the hem of her shorts, but it was
entirely pee- and baby-food free.

They'd eaten the sandwiches and shared the strawberry tart while he showed her the plans for the brewery and after he'd left her alone for a few minutes
so she could nurse Morgan, she'd gotten the carrier
from the car and strapped him onto her back, and
they'd walked over to the site where trenches for
underground plumbing and electrical were already
being dug.

In one direction, she'd been able to see the roof of
Stefan's farmhouse. In the other direction, the roof of

Treat Yourself with 2 Free Books!

GET UP TO 4 FREE BOOKS & 2 FREE GIFTS WORTH OVER $20

See Inside For Details

Claim up to FOUR NEW BOOKS & TWO MYSTERY GIFTS – absolutely FREE!

Dear Reader,

We both know life can be difficult at times. That's why it's important to treat yourself so you can relax and recharge once in a while.

And I'd like to help you do this by sending you this amazing offer of up to FOUR brand new full length FREE BOOKS that WE pay for.

This is everything I have ready to send to you right now:

Try **Harlequin® Special Edition** books featuring comfort and strength in the support of loved ones and enjoying the journey no matter what life throws your way.

Try **Harlequin® Heartwarming™ Larger-Print** books featuring uplifting stories where the bonds of friendship, family and community unite.

Or **TRY BOTH!**

All we ask in return is that you answer 4 simple questions on the attached Treat Yourself survey. You'll get **Two Free Books** and **Two Mystery Gifts** from each series you try, *altogether worth over $20*! Who could pass up a deal like that?

Sincerely,

Pam Powers

Harlequin Reader Service

Treat Yourself to Free Books and Free Gifts.

Answer 4 fun questions and get rewarded.

**We love to connect with our readers!
Please tell us a little about you...**

	YES	NO
1. I LOVE reading a good book.	◯	◯
2. I indulge and "treat" myself often.	◯	◯
3. I love getting FREE things.	◯	◯
4. Reading is one of my favorite activities.	◯	◯

TREAT YOURSELF • Pick your 2 Free Books...

Yes! Please send me my Free Books from each series I select and Free Mystery Gifts. I understand that I am under no obligation to buy anything, as explained on the back of this card.

Which do you prefer?

❑ **Harlequin® Special Edition** 235/335 HDL GRCC
❑ **Harlequin® Heartwarming™ Larger-Print** 161/361 HDL GRCC
❑ **Try Both** 235/335 & 161/361 HDL GRCN

FIRST NAME   LAST NAME

ADDRESS

APT.#   CITY

STATE/PROV.   ZIP/POSTAL CODE

EMAIL ❑ Please check this box if you would like to receive newsletters and promotional emails from Harlequin Enterprises ULC and its affiliates. You can unsubscribe anytime.

SE/HW-820-TY22

his partner's. In between was a pretty creek and the road from the highway that had already been paved and looked like a much straighter shot than the one that led to the farmhouse.

Morgan had slept through it all. Even when Stefan had helped remove him from the carrier and transfer him to the car seat in the back of her car.

She couldn't help feeling like those few brief moments had meant something to Stefan since he'd gone unusually quiet.

Maybe that was why she'd agreed when he'd told her that his family was anxious to meet the baby, and would she consider meeting them all one day soon?

"We could go to Provisions." He'd smiled coaxingly. "My sister-in-law Ashley wants to set it up. She's got the orange food thing down already."

She'd nodded. Morgan had more family than just her brothers and her mother. Family who—from the sounds of it at least—welcomed an addition to their ranks. "When?"

"How about Sunday afternoon?"

When she'd nodded again, he'd said he'd pick them up. And even when she'd said it was easier to meet him because of the car seat, he said he would come prepared.

So easily. Just like that.

Not that procuring a car seat was a difficult thing to do. People did it all the time.

Usually people who had more time to anticipate needing one than he'd had.

He hadn't said anything about seeing them again before Sunday. Which made her think that maybe he wanted a breather to absorb everything that had occurred over the last few days. She needed one, too.

She also needed a latte.

She'd been too busy with Stefan yesterday to stop at Kirby's Perks for her usual one. If she stopped now, maybe Kirby would be working and they could catch up.

She slowed in preparation of turning into the parking lot.

Through the plate glass window, she could see Bonita working alone at the counter. No sign of either Kirby or Hillary.

Justine flipped off her turn signal and sped up again.

She could fix a latte in her own apartment.

She was almost to her own block when she remembered that she was out of milk.

Get your head on straight, girl.

It was dark when she and Morgan came out of the grocery store with the milk plus several pouches of baby food and a postcard with a sepia-colored image of Rambling Rose when it still had a dirt road running through the center of town. She could give it to Martin.

Her breasts felt full and achy by the time she got

to her apartment. She stuck the milk in the fridge and sank down on the couch to feed Morgan.

He was ravenous, which was a good thing because she had a lot of milk.

She'd always had plenty.

Her mother had seemed scandalized by that. *After the first month, formula is the way to go, Justine. That's what I fed all of you. Are you trying to tell me I was wrong?*

She hadn't been trying to tell Kimberly anything of the sort, only that she didn't want her mom giving Morgan a supplemental bottle of formula when Justine wasn't looking. If she wanted to feed her grandson, then at least use Justine's breast milk.

Her thoughts drifted as she twirled her fingers through Morgan's glossy curls.

He'll need a haircut before he's a month old or people will think he's a girl, Justine.

He doesn't look anything like you, Justine.

If you had to go sleeping around with strangers, why on earth weren't you more careful, Justine?

She opened her eyes and willed the sound of her mom's voice back out of her head as she looked down at her son.

"You're way more beautiful than me," she whispered to him. "And we *were* careful, yet we still got you. My sweet baby boy."

He was oblivious, his eyes half rolling back in his head as he nursed. She was tired, too. She'd need that latte if she was going to make it through the work still waiting for her.

She closed her eyes for a moment. Stefan's Dolphins shirt was bunched up beneath her chin. It was probably her imagination that it smelled like him. When he'd come out with it for her, she'd recognized it from the folded stack that had been on the table in the laundry room.

She'd wash it and return it to him on Sunday when he came to pick them up.

She yawned again and scooched down a little more on the couch.

The knocking on her door startled her awake.

She couldn't have dozed off for long. Morgan hadn't finished nursing yet, though she could tell he was slowing down.

She rose, managing not to dislodge the baby, and walked over to the door. She peeked through the peephole and saw Gwen standing outside.

She opened the door. "Hi, Gwen. Come on in."

"Oh, sweetie." Gwen cooed at the sight of Morgan, and lightly rumpled his hair with her fingertips before bussing Justine's cheek with a light kiss. "I don't mean to disturb you this late, dear."

It was late enough that Justine figured she'd have to forgo Morgan's bath. But it was still barely seven. "It's not too late," she assured. "We just got a little off our usual routine." She went back and sat on the couch. "How've you been?"

"Fine. Fine. Just real fine." Instead of sitting, Gwen stood in the middle of the room.

Justine could see her gaze bouncing around.

"It's kind of a mess," she said, not really apologizing but feeling like she needed to say something.

"Don't be silly, dear. A person can't raise a baby in a tiny apartment and expect to have a place for everything and everything in its place." Gwen finally perched on the bar stool then stood again seconds later.

Justine felt a shiver of unease. Her landlady never had trouble sharing what was on her mind. "How's Debbie? I haven't talked to her in a couple weeks." She hadn't even told her yet about Stefan showing up in Rambling Rose.

"Oh, she's fine," Gwen said. She fussed with her hair for a moment and turned around again, clasping her hands at her waist. Her smile was over-bright.

That's when Justine noticed it.

The diamond ring on Gwen's left hand.

Morgan was heavy and limp in her arms. He was asleep, his pink lips parted. A drop of breast milk slowly crawling down his golden cheek.

She brushed it away and adjusted her bra. "Gwen," she asked slowly, "are you engaged?"

The older woman's smile turned tremulous. "I am."

Justine could only stare in wonder. "I hadn't even realized you were seeing someone special. You've had so many visitors lately." She stood with Morgan. "Let me put him down. Don't go anywhere. I want to hear all about it."

She went into the bedroom and slipped the baby into his crib. She leaned over to kiss his cheek before returning to the living area.

Gwen was still standing where she'd been, and Justine clasped her arm and drew her over to the couch. "When did this happen?"

"When I was on vacation." Gwen's cheeks looked flushed. "At least that's when I ran into Ron again. We knew each other in school, you see." She touched her hair again. "So long ago. It must sound silly."

Justine squeezed her hands. "I think it sounds wonderful," she assured. "And the ring is lovely. I can't believe I didn't notice it when you first got back from vacation!"

Gwen spread her fingers and the diamonds glinted in the light. "I didn't have it then. Ron just gave it to me a few days ago. He's been staying at the Hotel Fortune."

Justine raised her eyebrows. "Why not stay with you?"

"Oh, the Realtors. You know. They've been coming and going so often—" Gwen's lips pressed together, and her cheeks looked even redder. "The other day, three at once!"

"Realtors?"

Gwen took a deep breath. She tilted her head slightly and met Justine's eyes. "That's what I've been wanting to tell you. I'm selling the—well, I've *sold* the house. I'll be moving back to Minnesota with Ron."

She felt a sharp hitch in her chest. "Now I know it's true love," she managed lightly. "Moving back to snow country after saying how much you hated the cold."

This time it was Gwen who squeezed Justine's hands. "The new owner is going to keep renting to you, honey. He's agreed to that."

But without a lease, Justine knew that he could change his mind on a whim. There had just never been need for a lease between her and Gwen because of Debbie.

"Did you make a good profit on the sale at least?"

Gwen pressed her hand to her chest. "I can't even *tell* you how good. It's almost obscene. And *cash*. I was so worried I'd have to put on a new roof or something before I'd find a buyer, but this person didn't bat an eye. I was telling Mariana about it when I was at the Market and she thinks he's the same one who bought a house on her block last month."

Justine shored up her smile, but it took an effort. With every word that came out of Gwen's mouth, she could hear zeros getting added to her own rent. Especially if it was a real estate investor who'd bought Gwen's house.

"On top of all that cash, he plans to gut and remodel the entire house. Why, the man must be out of his mind, don't you think?"

"I think he's figured out what a lot of people have. That Rambling Rose is an up-and-coming town. And he was smart to offer you what he did."

Gwen laid her palm against Justine's cheek. "You're such a sweet girl. I knew you'd understand."

"What's not to understand?" She would fall apart later. "Romance finds a way."

"Particularly when you least expect it." Gwen giggled like she was a schoolgirl. "The wedding will be in Minnesota. You must promise to come. We haven't set the date yet, but in the next month or two."

"That soon?" Justine winced a little at the edge of panic she heard in her voice.

"I know. But we're both turning sixty-five this year. There's no reason to wait."

"And life's short," Justine murmured, thinking suddenly of Anika. She leaned forward and hugged Gwen. "I'm happy for you."

"I know you are, dear." Gwen squeezed her in return. When she sat back, her eyes were damp. "I'll be leaving with Ron tomorrow. We're driving. He's renting a trailer so I can take the few things from my house that I can't bear to part with. He has a daughter in Wichita and we'll stop there so we can meet. He wants to share our news with her in person."

"I'm sure she'll love you from the moment she meets you. But you're really only taking a few furnishings?"

"Not even furnishings. Just my piano and personal items. My Realtor is going to handle everything else before the new owner takes possession in a week—either selling or donating to charities. If there's anything you want, take it."

Justine was horrified how easily she pictured Gwen's Shaker sideboard in Stefan's family room. "I couldn't fit another thing up here," she said huskily, "but I appreciate the offer."

"I'll tell my Realtor about you anyway. Just in case. Then, if you change your mind, you'll have this weekend to deal with it. And I'll leave you the new owner's contact information so you can work out details."

Details that would undoubtedly include a higher rent.

Telling that to Gwen would be pointless though.

The woman was living her life. As she should.

The only one who needed to worry about Justine was Justine.

"Send me the wedding invitation," she said huskily. "Morgan and I will get there."

As if he'd heard his name, he suddenly let out a cry from the bedroom.

"Oh." Gwen's brow knitted. "We were too loud and woke him." She crept on her tiptoes to the door as if it would help the situation now. With her finger to her lips, she slipped quietly out the door and left.

Justine pinched her eyes closed for a moment, listening to the soft thumps on the staircase outside.

Then she went in to check on Morgan.

He had his butt in the air and his thumb in his

mouth. Whatever had disturbed him wasn't enough to wake him.

Justine leaned over, resting her arms on the rail of the crib as she watched him.

Maybe she should try sucking her thumb. See if it soothed away her troubles, too.

She didn't suck her thumb.

Nor did she curl up in bed and pull the covers over her head, tempting though it was.

Instead, she pulled up her big-girl panties and got on with it.

She fixed herself a latte and got her work done for the night. Her only indulgence was putting off the paper she still needed to finish for abnormal psych.

She could only handle one trauma at a time.

The next day she cleaned the apartment with extra care. She hadn't been on a lease, but she *had* paid first and last month's rent before she'd moved in. She didn't want to give the new owner any reason not to honor that.

She didn't want to contemplate that he might not legally have to.

On their way out with a covered trailer attached to the back of a dusty truck, Gwen introduced her to Ron and gave her a card with the new owner's information, plus a key to her house. "Remember," she said. "Take whatever you want."

Justine cried a little as she watched her landlady drive away. She knew she would lose it if she called

Debbie to congratulate her on acquiring a new uncle, so she sent a text message instead.

Debbie's response a few minutes later was typically brief.

See you at the wedding XOXO

There was nothing else to do in the apartment, so Justine buckled Morgan into his car seat. She had to stop at the gas station on their way to the Rambling Rose community hospital. She bought a few gallons of gas, added a few more pounds of air to her troublesome tire and picked up a colorful *ROSIE RENTALS!* magazine from the rack next to the newspapers.

Just in case.

When they arrived at the hospital to see Martin, Justine was pretty sure the only reason the nurses didn't make some protest over her rolling in with a baby and an enormous stroller was that they didn't expect the elderly man to survive.

Though she'd been afraid she'd find Martin hooked up to machines and tubes, he only had one IV running to his frail looking hand and one lead to a heart monitor.

He never opened his eyes. Never indicated in any way that he knew they were there. That he heard a single word she said as she talked about Gwen and the weather and her classwork and the fact that Morgan was growing increasingly mobile.

"I wish I could see you back at Kirby's Perks,

Martin," she said eventually. "You haven't met the new barista. It's ridiculous that I don't like her." It was horribly freeing. Unloading your thoughts on an unconscious listener. Someone who didn't argue with you or offer their own opinions or suggestions.

Nobody came into the room to interrupt their privacy. There were just the three of them and one machine that beeped softly and steadily.

She played him some songs on her phone that she knew he favored and filled him in on all the gossip that he'd missed. About the coffee shop and Kirby's recent engagement to Josh Fortune. "And talking about Fortunes. Mariana Sanchez is officially one of them now. Annette told me Mariana had a DNA test that proves it."

Martin's monitor suddenly bleeped, making Justine quickly cut off Etta James singing *At Last* on her phone even as a nurse hurried inside and checked it.

"Is he all right?"

The nurse nodded, and pressed a button and the monitor went silent again. "Just a blip. Happens occasionally." She smoothed Martin's bedding and left the room again.

Justine sat silently. Her heart eventually stopped skittering nervously. She picked at a ragged fingernail. "Stefan will be a great dad," she murmured. "I know he's angry that I didn't notify him right from the start that I was pregnant. And I know it's only been a few days, but he really doesn't seem to want to keep harping about it."

Morgan was asleep. He didn't stir when she moved him to the stroller.

She took out the sepia-toned postcard. "I brought you a postcard. It's a picture of Rambling Rose when it just had a dirt road." She propped it on the window ledge near the others that had been taped in place. It pained her slightly to realize the first one she'd sent him was of the Miami skyline. It was creased and bent and she soberly imagined him clutching it in his hand.

"I never told you about the first postcard I ever received. It came in the mail just before my fifth birthday." She rubbed her finger over one of the little strips of tape that was starting to come loose. "The picture on the front was of the Chatelaine courthouse. Sepia-colored just like this Rambling Rose one. The only thing handwritten on the back besides our address were the words *Happy Birthday*." She clasped her arms over her chest. "My mother always denied it, but I was certain, so certain that postcard came from my father. And here I am. Nineteen years later and still spending money on postcards that I never send to anyone."

She glanced at Martin in the bed. Her heart ached a little. Even though she only knew him through the coffee shop, he was a sweet old man. "Except for you." She leaned closer to him. "Aside from my mom," she confided in a whisper, "you're the only other one who knows my big secret."

If her brothers had ever even noticed her purchasing postcards now and then, she was certain they'd never attributed it to any specific reason.

She returned to her chair next to the bed just as the door opened and a different nurse this time entered. She checked the contents of the IV bag and the heart monitor and wrote her name on the white board affixed to the wall near the board and left again.

"I'm going to call the person who's buying Gwen's place, but I'm worried, Martin. I've seen how property values have been going up." She touched the handle of the stroller and jiggled it slightly. "Stefan might seem like the obvious way out, but—" She chewed the inside of her cheek. "There's nothing wrong with our life," she said after a moment. "One of these days I'll finish my graduate degree. Morgan will get older. He'll go to school. I'll have a job that pays more than just getting us by. Moving in with Stefan will get complicated. No matter what he says. I don't look at him and think logically. I look at him and think—" She exhaled.

Forever.

Not even there with Martin could she voice what felt so illogical. So improbable.

Nothing was forever.

She'd been taught that fact from the cradle.

She watched the droplets forming in the IV again. In the stroller beside her, Morgan snuffled and rolled over onto his back, his arms splayed. She knew he wouldn't sleep for much longer.

And he didn't.

She carefully leaned over the rails of Martin's hospital bed and kissed his lined cheek. "We all miss you," she whispered.

Then she pushed the stroller out of the room.

In one sense, her chest felt tighter than ever with emotion. In another, her mind felt clearer.

Confession. Good for the soul.

She drove back to the apartment and let Morgan loose on the floor while she left a voice mail for Gwen's new buyer.

"I'd like to discuss the lease of the garage apartment," she finished before hanging up. There was a snowball's chance that the owner wouldn't know she had no such lease, but what the heck.

The only time her phone made a peep after that, though, was when Stefan sent her a text message confirming the schedule for the following day.

It didn't require any more thought on her part than to reply that they'd be ready.

She ate a sandwich and fed Morgan bits of soft orange cheese and they entertained themselves for the rest of the day.

When it was bath time, she tried not to think too much about the claw-foot tub in the spacious bathroom at Stefan's. Tried even harder not to think about the bed in Stefan's room.

She put the baby down for the night and finished her psych paper, submitting it before the deadline by a record-breaking two hours.

She was in bed before midnight.

Her dreams were jumbled and it felt fitting that—for the first time in weeks—Morgan woke long before dawn with a pitiful wail.

She realized soon enough that he wasn't really hungry though. "You just want some company, don't you, bug?" She turned on some soft music and brought him to bed with her.

So what if it was salsa music?

He'd listened to it in the womb.

And it put him back to sleep now.

She, on the other hand, lay there remembering Stefan and the night they'd spent salsa dancing.

Remembering even more the next day when he'd kissed her—really kissed her, and softly asked if she was sure—really sure...

If a grain warehouse and a Belgian monastery had a baby, it would be Provisions. The gastronomic results make this a diamond in dining. Don't miss!

Reliving Stefan's lovemaking was too disturbing, and she'd finally crawled out of bed before dawn, and opened the rental brochure only to find the restaurant review printed on the back cover.

Aside from the glowing review, the brochure had held *no* affordable options for someone like Justine and she'd ended up tossing it in the trash. Then she'd opened her laptop and done her own share of chase-the-links down the webbernet.

By the time Stefan arrived to pick up her and Morgan that afternoon, not only had she pored over the

Mendoza Winery website again, but she'd also read more about the three sisters who'd founded Provisions and she knew the menu by heart.

When a stunning blonde greeted Stefan and Justine at the entrance of the restaurant, she knew it was Ashley Fortune Mendoza even before Stefan introduced them.

"I'm so pleased to meet you," Ashley greeted warmly. "I *love* your dress."

Justine managed to control her sudden urge to fuss with the purple dress that had been a Christmas gift from Debbie and Todd. It was long and sleeveless with a scooped neck that was a little lower than she would have liked, but it was a lot more stylish than her usual clothing.

In the face of Ashley's chic eyelet sheath, Justine was glad that she'd finally torn off the tags and steamed out the wrinkles from being crammed in her closet for six months. "I love yours," she returned truthfully. The only other person she knew who'd have the panache for such a dress was Garland.

"And this, obviously, is Morgan." Ashley clapped her hands together and held them toward the baby.

"He isn't used to strangers," Stefan said before Justine could offer her usual warning.

"That's okay." Ashley immediately dropped her hands and just leaned forward until she was at Morgan's level. "We're family, aren't we, handsome? We won't be strangers for long."

Morgan, amazingly enough, stared right back into her long-lashed eyes as if fascinated.

"Come on." Ashley tucked her arm through Stefan's and drew them through the busy restaurant. "I've set us up in the wine cellar. I figured it would be a little more private."

Justine managed a smile that she hoped didn't look as nervous as she felt. She'd read that Ashley and her sisters had been a year younger than Justine was now when they'd started the restaurant. It was hard not to feel a little intimidated now in the face of the woman's ambition.

"Watch your step," Ashley warned as they stepped through an arched doorway at the end of the bar. "The stairway is a little narrow."

It wasn't as narrow as the one at Stefan's house.

He went ahead of Justine, though, looking back often as if he was prepared to catch her if she lost her step.

"We're fine." The sconces on the stone walls flickered like gas lamps but they offered plenty of light. And if her grip was white-knuckled on the wrought iron railing, it had a lot more to do with nerves over meeting Stefan's family than it did navigating the steps.

When they reached the bottom, they entered a spacious room with brick walls. Horizontal racks loaded with wine bottles stretched from the ceiling to a brick floor partially covered by an enormous Persian rug that—considering what Justine had read during her webbernet dive into the vast Fortune family—was probably *not* a reproduction. The trestle table could seat at least a dozen people—which was good, because it looked like there were nearly that many clustered around the spacious room.

Goose bumps popped out on her shoulders.

"Here." Stefan immediately shrugged out of his linen jacket. He was wearing a short-sleeved collarless black shirt beneath. Under any other circumstances, she'd have called it a T-shirt, but one glance was enough to know it wasn't anything so mundane. It was probably silk spun from hand-fed caterpillars on some exotic mountaintop. His jacket was large enough to encompass her and Morgan and she automatically clasped it together with her free hand.

No imagination this time. The jacket *did* smell like Stefan. It was all she could do not to bury her nose in it.

His hand lightly touched her back as they walked deeper into the room.

The men immediately stood. They all looked strikingly similar. Garland hadn't been whistling Dixie. The Mendoza genes were *good*.

And one day, her son was going to stand just as tall and handsome.

"Rodrigo," Stefan said when one of them stepped forward and slid his arm around Ashley's shoulder. "And that's Mark and Megan."

She smiled and nodded. Megan wasn't quite an identical replica of Ashley. In a pencil skirt and silk blouse, she was less flamboyant. She, too, had a man's jacket over her shoulders. Her husband's, obviously. "We're so pleased to meet you," she said. "I see my sister didn't warn y'all about the wine cellar any more than she warned us."

"What's the fun in life if you can't wear your man's jacket when you're chilly?" Ashley waved a graceful hand and the diamonds on her finger winked in the light. "We do have sweaters," she offered. "If that's more your speed."

Justine almost wished they didn't. She looked at Stefan questioningly. "Do you want your jacket—"

"If we don't have enough orange food this afternoon, better to clean my jacket than one of Ashley's five-hundred-dollar sweaters."

"Oh, you." Ashley looked at Justine and rolled her eyes. "I'm sure you've already realized how prone to exaggeration these Mendoza men are. Particularly the ones who specialize in marketing. But I hope Morgan's going to be warm enough."

"He'll be fine," Justine assured. She had plenty of clothes in the backpack that Stefan was still holding. Right now, he was cozy enough in stretchy pants that looked like jeans and a pullover shirt patterned to look like a vest and bow tie. She'd even managed to comb his wayward curls into some semblance of order.

He'd had his morning nap and she'd nursed him right before Stefan picked them up. Barring accidents, she figured they were set for at least two hours.

"Well, if he needs anything at all, you just let us know." Ashley swept her hair over her shoulder. It was the kind of blond that Justine's had never been. Bright and thick and sporting long, loose waves.

The Fortunes had genes as blessedly beautiful as the Mendozas.

"Talking about exaggeration, Ashley, when you organized this meet-the-fam deal, I thought it was just going to be the Rambling Rose crew." Stefan looked at Justine as he gestured. "That's my brother Carlo."

"The oldest," Ashley provided sotto voce.

"The smartest," Carlo corrected, hearing her perfectly well. He gave Stefan a bear hug and shook Justine's hand. "Schuyler, my wife, wanted to be here but she was caught up in a real estate thing."

Schuyler was one of the Fortunados, Justine knew. Another branch of the family, courtesy of some old guy who'd liked to fool around a lot. He'd left a trail of offspring from New York to Florida to who knew where. Ashley and Megan's side of the Fortunes hailed from Florida, but the Fortunados were the ones heavily into Texas real estate.

Too bad they couldn't solve Justine's present real estate worry.

"And this is Chaz—" another bear hug ensued "—and Savannah." Stefan squeezed his sister-in-law right off her feet. "You guys should have told me you were coming. Are you heading back to Austin today or staying over?"

"Staying over at Hotel Fortune," Savannah said. She had long dark hair and a distinctive southern drawl, and she gave Justine a quick wink. "Nothing like hotel sex to liven up—" Her husband smiled and pressed his hand lightly over her mouth.

Justine bit her lip, holding back an unexpected laugh. They were all too friendly and engaging not to like right off the bat. "I'm Texas born and bred. That's not a Texas drawl you have."

"New Orleans," Savannah said, pulling away her husband's hand.

"Sweetest branch of ol' Julius Fortune," Chaz said.

"Good thing Schuyler's not here to hear that," Carlo commented. "She might take exception."

"You're joking, right?" Justine looked from Ashley and Megan to Savannah. "You're *all* related? Not just because of marriage?"

"Savannah's married to a Mendoza," Ashley drawled humorously. "So, of course, she's a Fortune. We all are of one sort or another. Mendozas marry Fortunes. Kind of turning into a deal."

"Speak for yourselves," Stefan said abruptly. His green gaze found Justine's, pointedly.

She swallowed.

It took much, much too long before she was finally able to look away.

Chapter Eight

"I don't know if I should be worried or not." Rodrigo threw himself down on the chair next to Stefan's.

Dinner was over and now an array of desserts sat on the long table waiting for anyone to partake when they were ready.

Right now, all the women were clustered around Ashley, who was bouncing Morgan on her hip while Justine sat nearby, a bemused look on her face. She'd finally exchanged his jacket for one of the flowy sweaters that Ashley had brought. It was a little too big for her. Not as big as his jacket.

He'd known she was nervous when they'd first arrived, but there didn't seem to be any sign of it now.

He figured that had more to do with his sisters-in-law than anything else.

He belatedly remembered his brother and glanced Rodrigo's way. "Worried about what?"

"The look on my wife's face while she's holding Morgan."

"At least you'd be married," Stefan muttered and lifted the cup of coffee that he'd switched to after dinner.

Chaz joined them. "Who'd be married?"

Stefan wished he'd kept his thought to himself. "Nobody." He pretended not to see the look passing between his brothers.

"How's the brewery coming?" Carlo asked as he perused the desserts. "How're you managing to juggle everything now?"

His juggling was nothing compared to what Justine dealt with every day.

"It's fine. Unless you're in a hurry to get back to Austin you should come by and see the property. We've got the foundation for the main building staked out. They'll start working on it this week." There was nothing special to show off about the house.

Except the claw-foot tub. She nearly drooled over it.

He wondered if any man ever had bribed a woman under his roof with a tub that had to be at least eighty years old.

Across the room, Justine had jumped off her chair as if startled.

He automatically looked toward Morgan, but the baby was fine. His stranger-danger instincts had evidently been conquered by the lovely women doting over him.

Smart boy.

Stefan wished he could take some of the credit.

He looked back toward Justine just in time to see her walking out of the room, her cell phone at her ear.

He set down his coffee cup. "Be back." He pushed out of his chair and followed her.

She'd stopped halfway up the stairs. Her hand was clutching her honey-blond hair away from her face as she leaned against the wall. "That's double what I'm paying now!" Her voice was clearly audible.

Plainly agitated.

Stefan must have made a sound because she suddenly turned and looked down at him.

In the flickering light from the sconces, he could see her shoulders slump slightly.

The look of defeat on her face made him want to punch something. Preferably the person on the other side of the phone call. But when he grasped the wrought iron handrail and put his foot on the bottom step, she held up her hand.

It went against the grain, but he stopped. He did not go back into the wine cellar though. Screw privacy.

"I understand," she said into the phone. "And you understand that I'll expect my last month's rent returned?" She listened for a moment. "Yes. I appreciate you letting me know so quickly."

She didn't particularly sound appreciative.

And she didn't say another word to the caller either. Just hung up and slid the phone into a hidden pocket of her dress.

Her dress wasn't any more revealing than what his sisters-in-law were wearing. In fact, considering it reached to her ankles, it covered a helluva lot more.

He'd still spent way too much time thinking—remembering—what was beneath.

He dragged his thoughts back up above his belt. It was a frequent chore lately. "What's wrong?"

She looked pale, but that could be attributed to the light. "I thought I'd have a few more days before—" She broke off and shook her head. Her lashes lowered for a moment as if she was gathering strength. When they lifted again, her caramel eyes were shimmering. "My landlady sold her house and my rent just got doubled. So." She cleared her throat softly. "If that offer's still open—"

He took two stairs before he realized it and made himself stop again. From the wine cellar he could hear his brothers and their wives talking, accompanied by the music of Morgan's hiccupping laughter.

"*Which* offer?" he asked slowly.

Her lips pressed together. He tracked the progress of her swallow down her long, lovely throat. It was a short trip from there to the creamy skin exposed by the low scoop of her dress.

"The second one," she finally said. "Obviously."

Right now, he wasn't sure what was obvious or not. Except that his pulse felt like it was ready to explode out of his head. "You and Morgan will live with me."

"We'll move into your house," she said, as if there was supposed to be some difference. Her lashes dropped again. "I'll pay you the same rent—"

"No."

"—that I paid Gwen." She looked at him again. The glistening was waning. "It's not negotiable, Stefan. It's not a lot of money but it's the only thing that's going to keep me from feeling like a charity case. If you won't take rent from me, I'll—"

"What? Cough up twice as much to stay where you are?" He took two more steps toward her. Made himself stop again. "You're the mother of my *son*, Justine. In what universe does wanting to provide for you both equate to charity?"

"I can't stop you from providing for Morgan. That's different than—"

"Stop. Or I'm going to get seriously pissed off."

She pressed her lips together again. But her chin came up in that way he was beginning to recognize.

Nothing was going to be solved if they were at a stalemate.

"How much?" he asked more or less calmly. "How much were you paying Gwen?"

"Five hundred dollars."

Which meant the new owner planned to get

a thousand. For a few hundred square feet atop a damned garage.

He tightened his grip on the railing until the urge to say what he really thought about that passed. Real estate investment was one thing.

Gouging, another.

"Do you have student loans?" He'd bet his soul on it.

She nodded.

"Put your five hundred toward the loans," he said. "Consider it an investment in our son's future," he added when she opened her mouth to protest again.

Her gaze flickered and her lips pressed together for a long moment. "I don't want a nanny," she said eventually, taking another tack entirely.

"Okay." That one was easy. He knew he'd already won the round.

"And you probably don't need a housekeeper," she added. "Unless you've already hired one. I wouldn't want to put someone out of a job or anything."

"I've already hired one," he lied steadily. He could find someone. Make sure they knew the value of discretion.

Her lips rounded in a soft "Oh." Then she was just silent again.

He knew she could hear Morgan laughing in the room below them as well as he could.

"Does that bother you?" He jerked his chin. "That he's momentarily okay without you right beside him?"

Her lips stretched into a faint curve that was damned-near heartbreaking. "I think what bothers me more is that I've never heard him laugh around *my* brothers." She drew in a deep, shuddering breath that lifted her chest and made him look away.

Yeah, he wanted her to his back teeth, and he was probably going to get old before his time knowing she was sleeping in a bedroom a few doors away from him and was off limits. But he hadn't been raised to focus on the short-term gain at the cost of the true reward.

Whether it was fate or divine intervention or just a chaotic universe, they were all here now. At the same place. In the same time.

He wasn't going to squander it by letting basic desire get in the way.

And even as he thought it, he heard his brothers laugh heartily.

He raked his fingers through his hair and focused on her right ear. She'd tucked her hair behind it again. It was an exceptionally lovely ear but not as distracting as her eyes. Or her mouth. Or every other inch of her.

He blew out a breath and lifted his gaze to the lamp above her head, instead. "When's the last time they saw him?"

"Who?"

She was obviously as distracted as he was. "Your brothers."

"They came to see him when he was born. I think

we should probably rejoin the others," she added abruptly.

He didn't want to judge too quickly but there was obviously a big difference between her brothers and his. His were in his business every time he turned around. Occasionally it was a pain in the ass. But the bottom line was they were his best friends.

"How soon do you need to be out of your apartment?"

She shrugged. "The sooner the better, I suppose. The new owner takes possession in a week. Gwen told me he plans to gut the place." Her lips thinned. "Maybe he'll gut the apartment, too."

"Then start packing tomorrow. I'll bring boxes." And muscle. Another useful purpose where brothers were concerned.

"Stefan."

A ripple worked down the base of his spine. He focused harder on the wall sconce. "Yeah?"

"Tell me we're not digging a bigger hole for ourselves."

"We're not digging a bigger hole for ourselves," he repeated without missing a beat. He looked at her then. Her eyes were wide. Worried. "It'll be okay. You can trust me. This isn't about you or me. Morgan's the point here."

She didn't look convinced. But she nodded. "Morgan's the point," she repeated.

He noticed she didn't say squat about trust.

Probably smart. Even though he was a man of his

word, who in the world ever trusted someone who said "trust me"?

He backed down the steps he'd climbed. "Dessert's in there. If I remember right, you like crème brûlée." He wanted to kick himself. They'd shared that dessert the night they'd met.

She didn't seem to be thinking about that though. "I do." She lifted the long folds of her dress slightly and descended the stairs toward him.

He could either stand there and let her bump against him or move aside.

Trust me.

Somewhere inside his head, laughter was directed squarely at himself.

He asked her to trust him and he wasn't even sure he could trust himself.

Not where she was concerned.

"Grab that end of the couch."

That was Mark. Justine could pick out the differences between Stefan's brothers' voices now.

"I've *got* the end of it," Stefan said, sounding excessively patient. "Just turn it— No, not that way."

Laughter—definitely with a mocking edge— belonged to Rodrigo. *"Pivot!"*

Justine didn't bother trying to muffle her laugh. She was boxing up the contents of her chest of drawers in her bedroom. The guys in her living room, doing their best to maneuver her couch out the door and down the stairs, would never even hear her.

Not with all the grunting and good-natured squabbling and occasional swearing they'd been doing.

They'd arrived a little over an hour ago and had already nearly emptied the bedroom. The only thing from her room yet to take down to the trailer that was attached to the back of Stefan's pickup truck was the crib—currently occupied by Morgan who was lying on his back and sucking on his toes.

She was leaving her narrow bed and the chest of drawers in the apartment, which was why she was emptying it.

Gwen had told her to take whatever she wanted from her house, and so she did.

The Shaker sideboard from Gwen's dining room. And two full bedroom suites. One for herself. One for Morgan.

She had phoned the real estate agent just to make sure she wasn't overstepping her bounds.

"Most of that old stuff's just going to get donated anyway," he'd said. "Knock yourself out."

Justine shook her head. The care that had gone into the craftsmanship of that *old stuff* exceeded a lot of furniture being made nowadays.

The guys were still bickering as they finally succeeded in manhandling the couch out of the apartment when she went to take a look.

None of them noticed her.

Which was good. So far, they hadn't made a big deal about her moving in with Stefan.

"Moving into his *house*," she corrected herself.

It was a fine delineation.

If she said it often enough, would it become second nature?

Or an even bigger lie?

She returned to the bedroom. Morgan had tired of his toes and had pulled himself up to standing while he yanked on the bars of the crib. She picked up the toy keys that he'd tossed onto the floor and handed them to him. "Almost done, bug."

The keys sailed out again and he chortled. Penned up or not, he was having a grand time.

She tossed the keys back in the crib before pulling out the bottom drawer and finished stuffing the contents into the packing box. It was already overstuffed. She'd never get the flaps closed. But it wasn't as if they were transporting things across country.

She went into the bathroom with the one remaining empty box and could hear the guys returning.

"—you know how persistent Belle can be," Rodrigo was saying. "She read the whole book that Josh received as if it would explain the anonymous gifts they've all been getting."

"It's just a tourism book of Texas." Stefan sounded dismissive.

"You've gotta admit it's all pretty curious." That was Mark. "Yeah, the gifts led to them all realizing Mariana Sanchez is actually a member of the Fortune family, but it does seem like a roundabout way of doing it. Why not send an anonymous gift directly to Mariana? Instead, Belle gets the rose print.

Brian finds the safe deposit key in the horse statue that Brady and Harper received which leads to the poem written by MAF—"

"It wasn't written by MAF. The initials just referred to Mariana. Mary Anne Fortune," Rodrigo said. "Then there was the blanket that Beau received. And the vinyl record that Draper got—"

"You've both been listening too much to Belle," Stefan said. "You'd think she'd have enough to concentrate on with her new fiancé."

Justine recognized Rodrigo's laugh. "Much to your relief considering the way she first set her sights on *you*."

"Are we here to gossip or move furniture," Mark interrupted over Stefan's muttered "shut up."

Justine quickly began boxing items from under the sink when she heard footsteps nearing. She knew it was Stefan before he even spoke.

"You nearly finished in here?"

"Just about." She glanced at his reflection in the mirror before leaning over the bathtub to scoop up Morgan's bath toys. She'd heard enough gossip at Kirby's Perks to know that Belle was a Fortune, too, who'd moved to Rambling Rose from New Orleans. But now all she could think about was her apparent interest in Stefan. "I'm on the last box. The one in the bedroom is ready. I can take it in my car though. It's too full to close up."

"What about the ice chest on the kitchen counter?"

"It's milk."

"We can buy milk, Justine."

"Not this milk," she said pointedly. She'd packed all the ice in her freezer around the bags of breast milk, but the ice chest was a cheap Styrofoam thing she'd found in the garage.

"Got it." He looked vaguely disconcerted. "Let me know when you're ready for us to take apart the crib."

"I'm ready." It wasn't true, but that was beside the point.

He nodded and disappeared again and after a moment, the apartment was silent again except for Morgan's jabbering.

She took the towels from the rack and tucked them around the toiletries and toys and carried the box into the bedroom. The overfull box was already gone.

She took the last box out to the living area, set it on the floor near the door and returned to the bedroom.

Morgan's diaper was still dry and she lifted him out of the crib.

The closet was empty, and the walls were blank. Aside from the crib, nothing was left but a bare mattress on a frame and a cheap chest with drawers that stuck whenever the humidity was high.

She didn't expect to feel choked up.

But she did.

"Ready for us to take the crib?"

She startled slightly. Mark's eyebrows were raised questioningly. She gave a quick nod and scooped up

Morgan's blanket and toys from the crib before moving out of the way.

She'd had to assemble the crib inside the bedroom, which meant it had to be disassembled again to get it out. She was glad the guys had just assumed they'd take care of it.

Chauvinistic on their part? Perhaps.

But she was glad anyway. It had taken her a full day to put together—with her eldest brother, Lincoln, watching and advising during an intensely frustrating video call.

Rodrigo entered the room only long enough to grab the mattress that Mark easily lifted out of the crib, and then Stefan appeared with a small red toolbox in his hand.

She ducked her chin and carried Morgan out to the living room. The room was entirely empty.

The couch had left dents in the thin carpet. The wall where her postcard canvas had hung still had the same visible drywall patch that had been there when she'd first moved in.

The knot was growing inside her chest.

She shouldered the backpack and carried Morgan outside and down the stairs. The box from the bathroom had already disappeared.

Outside, Stefan's trailer was backed up to the garage. He and his brothers had stacked the furniture inside it like some three-dimensional puzzle. She couldn't imagine where he'd find room to put the crib, even once it was taken apart.

She dumped the backpack in the front seat of her car. In the back next to Morgan's car seat, she could see the last two boxes she'd packed. She pulled out a few of the bath toys for Morgan and then sat down on the grass so he could crawl around.

After spending the last hour in confinement, he was raring to go.

When she heard footsteps on the stairs, she braced herself to see the crib coming out in pieces.

But Stefan wasn't carrying anything, and he came over to where they were sitting in the grass.

Not even the distracting sight of the small screwdriver he'd tucked behind his ear like a pencil was enough to make her forget Rodrigo's comment about Belle being interested in Stefan. "Problem with the crib?"

"Not once we found a video online showing how to take it apart," he admitted wryly.

She smiled despite herself. "Putting it together was an adventure, too."

"I bet." He crouched next to her and removed the screwdriver, jabbing the pointed end lightly into the grassy earth. "You're sad leaving here."

She'd thought she'd conquered the prickling behind her eyes. "It's just an apartment."

He was silent.

Waiting.

"All but a couple weeks of Morgan's life have been spent here." Her breath hitched.

His hand lightly touched hers. His fingernails

were clipped short. He had a scrape on one knuckle. Small but fresh. Earned that afternoon, helping to dismantle her home.

Belle was engaged to someone else, she reminded herself. Maybe she'd been interested in Stefan but no woman in her right mind would choose someone else if he'd set his interest on her in return.

She looked away from the scraped knuckle and pretended she didn't have a shocking urge to kiss the scrape.

And maybe he knew, because he drew back his hand and plucked the screwdriver out of the ground again. "It was hard when I left Miami." He rolled the tool between his palms. "It's hard to leave your home."

The apartment *had* been home. Haven.

She missed it already and she hadn't even locked the door for the final time.

"Why did you?" she asked.

The sunlight made his eyes seem lighter than usual. More like sea glass from a Florida beach than moss from a forest glen.

"I was ready." He shrugged one shoulder. "My brothers were in Texas. My dad was gone more often than not."

"Your mom?"

"We're not close."

"I'm sorry."

"It's nobody's fault. She's got her life and she's happy. She wasn't always. So." His lips tilted. "There's that. We talk on holidays. Birthdays. That sort of thing."

She wished she felt as much equanimity where both her parents were concerned.

Morgan was scooting through the grass, earning grass stains on his romper as he aimed for a huge butterfly that was sunning itself on Gwen's rose-bushes. She scooped him up before he got too close to the bush and noticed that Mark was subtly peering around the corner of the apartment doorway at the top of the stairs.

She drew in another deep breath.

"You can tell Mark it's safe to bring down the crib now," she told Stefan.

He smiled slightly as he rose. "And the ice chest full of milkcicles?"

She nodded and watched him jog up the steps. Tall. Lithe. Wavy dark hair gleaming under the sunshine.

She knew she would miss the apartment.

But she was more afraid that she wouldn't miss it for long.

Chapter Nine

"Get you another burger?"

Justine smiled ruefully and waved off the offer. "I'm already stuffed, Laurel, but thanks."

"So am I," Laurel admitted with a wry laugh.

Justine figured the other woman was more than a few years older than her, but only because of the way she and Adam talked about their college days when Stefan had mentioned Justine was working on her graduate degree.

"Not that us all being stuffed stops my husband from stoking the coals in the barbecue over there," Laurel added as she sank into the lawn chair next to Justine. "Looks like those two are done in for the night, too." She nodded toward the blanket that was spread on the grass.

Morgan was sprawled on his back, sound asleep. So was his blanket-mate Larkin. Even though the toddler was two years older than Morgan, the cute little boy had been fascinated with the baby and hadn't moved more than a few feet away from him since he and his parents showed up at Stefan's house.

"We're barging in whether you want us here or not," Adam had said.

"We know what moving day is like," Laurel had added. "So we've brought food and drink and just enough energy to get us all through dinner, at which point we promise to go away as quickly as we appeared."

Justine had liked them both just as much as she'd liked Stefan's brothers and their wives.

Plus, Adam and Laurel's unexpected appearance helped dispel the awkward feeling that had begun building the minute Mark and Rodrigo left after unloading the trailer.

She had no clue if Stefan felt similarly relieved by his business partner's arrival. The two men had talked nonstop brewery stuff the whole evening, leaving Justine and Laurel to fill the gap.

Fortunately, they were both moms. The conversation never lagged for that reason, alone.

"We're having Adam's brothers over to our place next weekend for a pool party. We'd love it if you came as well," Laurel said now. "You'll have had a chance to settle in here a bit, and Adam's been wanting to show off the house now that we're finally settled in."

"Where'd you live before?"

"We were using one of the guest houses over at Callum's. Have you met?"

Justine shook her head. "I've heard of him, of course. How he was responsible for developing the pediatric center." His wife was one of the nurses there. "I've met Becky, though, when I've had to take Morgan there."

Laurel nodded. "Right. Well, Callum's one of Adam's cousins." She hesitated as if she expected some comment from Justine.

Was Justine supposed to know that? She'd lived in town long enough to know you couldn't swing a cat without hitting someone named Fortune. But how they were all related would take a cartographer.

Her gaze drifted to Stefan. What she hadn't expected was the proliferation of Mendozas.

As if he felt her attention, he looked up from the stack of blueprints he'd retrieved from inside the house. He and Adam both had the flashlight apps on their cell phones turned on and directed at the drawings spread across the picnic table, and even though she couldn't read his expression, she suddenly felt shaky inside.

She quickly focused on the woman beside her. "We had dinner with Stefan's brothers at Provisions yesterday."

"Then you've met Ashley and Savannah and Schuyler, too."

"Not Schuyler. She couldn't make it."

"Counting Adam and them, you've already met four different branches of the mighty Fortune tree."

"The invasive Fortune *weed*," Adam said, obviously overhearing.

"You sound like your dad," Laurel told him.

"I take it back," he said immediately. "Mighty tree. *Mighty*."

Laurel's eyes danced even in the dim light as she looked toward Justine again. "Adams's dad's never been delighted over learning he's part of the larger sphere spawned indiscriminately by Julius Fortune," she explained. "Gary would pull up every tree root if he could."

She didn't look particularly bothered by it, nor did Adam look particularly bothered by his wife's opinion regarding his father.

Morgan snuffled and rolled over, realized immediately that he was in unfamiliar territory and let out a wail. Justine went over to pick him up. He'd eaten a healthy share of sweet potatoes that had been already cubed and roasted when Laurel took them out, which made Justine highly suspicious that Stefan had prepped his partner, despite the apparent spontaneity of them "dropping by with dinner." Now, though, he'd need nursing.

And a bath.

The commotion woke up Larkin, too, who knuckled his eyes as he trotted over to his mother. "Baby cwying, Mama."

"He's hungry," Justine told him. "So, I'm going to go inside and feed him."

"I come?"

"Not this time," Laurel told him. "It's late and about time for daddy and me to take *you* home." She stood and swung him so that his legs flopped from one side to the other and he giggled. Over his head, she gave Justine a quick smile. "We'll be in touch about next weekend."

Justine quickly carried Morgan inside and felt distinctly rattled when Stefan followed. He turned on the inside light and she blinked under its intrusive glare.

"You have everything you need?" he asked.

She didn't welcome the nervous fluttering inside her. "I'm just going to feed him." She sounded sharper than the situation warranted and forced a calming breath. "Sorry. I'm fine. We're fine." She forced a smile. "Have boobs, will travel."

The humor felt flat as a pancake.

"I'll turn on some light," he said, walking ahead of her as if he couldn't wait to get her moving on her way. A moment later, light washed the walls of the hallway, illuminating the narrow stairwell.

"It won't take long to feed him," she said.

"Even if it did, you don't have to rush," he assured, making her even more certain that he hoped she *didn't* return too quickly.

Meanwhile, Morgan was pulling at her T-shirt more impatiently than ever. "Mamaaaaa!"

She could have sat on her own old couch that had been placed in the parlor and nursed Morgan. But with Stefan lingering nearby, she headed up the stairs.

Her rocking chair was in Morgan's bedroom next to the one she'd chosen for herself—directly across from the bathroom with the claw-foot tub.

She nudged the bedroom door closed with her foot and crossed to the chair. She fed Morgan, who fell asleep before he really finished, and she gave up the idea of a bath for him and just put him down in his crib.

Now that it was done, she wasn't sure at all about her decision not to place the crib in her bedroom. Unlike at the apartment, there was plenty of room here.

What if he cried in the night and she didn't hear him?

She heard a creak of wood floor in the hallway and glanced at the door. She'd thought she'd closed it, but it obviously hadn't latched. She could see Stefan through the few inches where it had drifted open.

She crossed the room and stepped into the hallway. "He's asleep," she whispered.

Stefan handed her a gift bag. "From Adam and Laurel." He whispered, too. "They forgot it in their car."

This bag was a lot heavier than the one that had

contained Stefan's earlier gift of the plastic keys. "What is it?"

He lifted his palms. "Open it and see."

She left the door to the bedroom wide open and tiptoed back toward the stairs.

The floor still creaked.

What she'd found a comforting sound a few days ago now echoed like a sure way to disturb a sleeping baby.

She stopped at the head of the steps where the jar-shaped light fixture in the ceiling illuminated the stairwell, and pulled out the glossy box nestled in tissue. She turned it toward the light to study the colored picture on the front.

Stefan's shoulder brushed against her as he leaned closer to see it, too. "Baby monitor. Handy."

Until tonight, Laurel and Adam didn't know her from, well, Adam. But they'd been thoughtful enough to give her a gift that was so ideally perfect, it made her eyes flood with tears.

He lifted the box out of her nerveless fingers and turned the box over. "D'you know how it works?"

She wondered if he was even aware of the hand he'd dropped on her shoulder. "I ought to, but I never needed a monitor in the apartment."

"Camera goes where Morgan is and you can watch it from an app on your computer or smartphone from wherever you are. Says it senses movement and changes of temperature and sends notifications to the app. Seems simple enough." He slit the plastic encasing the box with his fingernail. "Want to set it up now?"

She nodded.

"Downstairs," he suggested. "Better light."

She nodded again. Her throat was too tight to speak.

Maybe he knew, because he squeezed her shoulder lightly and then dropped his hand before heading down the stairs.

She waited for her breathing to slow but gave it up as a lost cause and started after him.

She found her glasses and sat next to him on the couch in the family room while he pulled out the instructions. In a matter of minutes, the view from the camera—currently aimed at his forehead as he studied its workings—showed on the screen of her cell phone.

She zoomed in to the small scar on his left eyebrow.

"How'd you get it?"

His eyebrow rose as he glanced at her.

She lifted her hand, realized she was about to touch his eyebrow and showed him the phone instead. "The scar?"

"Bicycle accident. Went straight over the handlebars. Landed on a rock."

"You're lucky you didn't put out an eye."

His teeth flashed. "Exactly what my mom said, only at the top of her lungs. I'd been riding where I wasn't allowed."

Her stomach swooped from that smile. "I guess all moms think alike."

He handed her the camera and she stood.

She could see through the windows that the picnic table had been cleared away. The lawn chairs were folded and stacked on top of it. "Laurel and Adam are nice."

The leather couch creaked when he stood, also. "They are."

"She mentioned—"

"They want us—"

They both broke off.

Stefan waved his hand, then pushed it into his front pocket. "You go."

"It's nothing. Just that Laurel mentioned dinner with them next weekend."

His lips twitched. "Adam told me the same thing."

She was starting to feel awkward again. She chewed the inside of her cheek, glancing at him from the corners of her eyes. "It's been quite a day."

"Yes." His other hand went into his other pocket.

"I think I'll head up."

"Sure." He looked down. Rocked on his boots. "I've got some work to take care of."

So did she, but it was going to have to wait until she could think, and right now her thoughts were too scrambled. "Thanks for everything today."

"I don't want thanks." His gaze lifted, the seaglass eyes warm and mossy again. "If you need anything—"

"I'm sure we'll be fine. Appearances to the contrary, I really *am* used to taking care of myself and Morgan." She forced a smile. "My brothers were always a unit. I was the only girl. Taught me early on to rely on myself."

He didn't smile though. "I was going to say that if you needed anything, let me know. But maybe I should just tell you to poke around until you find it."

She exhaled a half laugh.

"I'm still living out of boxes, too," he reminded.

"Right." She tucked her hair behind her ear. Silly to forget that, when the evidence was all around her. "Well. Good night."

"G'night, Justine."

She left the room at a respectably calm pace. As soon as she reached the privacy of the stairwell, however, she leaned against the wall, pressing her cell phone against her racing heart.

She *really* needed to get a grip. They hadn't even been there for twelve hours.

"Just staying in the same house," she whispered to herself. "That's it." She straightened. Inhaled slowly. Exhaled even slower. "Nothing more."

Despite her worries, Justine slept like a stone that night.

She'd placed the baby monitor on the dresser from Gwen's house which was positioned opposite Morgan's crib, and tested the view of him on her phone from her bedroom. With the sound turned up, she'd been able to hear every rustle he made, and she'd relaxed a little over the idea of him sleeping so far away from her.

She'd washed up in the bathroom with her phone sitting on top of the narrow glass shelf above the towel rack.

She wasn't relaxed enough to take a bath, but that had nothing to do with Morgan and everything to do with his daddy.

Closed in the privacy of her new bedroom—where she'd made certain the door *did* latch—she made up her new bed with sheets from Gwen's linen closet. They smelled clean and vaguely of lavender. She needed to remember to send Gwen a thank-you note for everything.

She'd been too tired to unpack the rest of her stuff from the two suitcases and a black lawn-and-leaf bag. Not too tired, though, to avoid the temptation of wearing Stefan's Dolphin's T-shirt to bed. Instead, she changed into yoga shorts and a camisole, propped her phone on the nightstand where she could easily see the screen and fell asleep watching the blue-gray image of Morgan sleeping on the other side of the wall.

When she woke the next morning, it was to the sound of his happy babbles.

The image on her phone was full of daylight and color.

He was standing in his crib, chewing on the top rail and bouncing.

Delighted and curious as to how long it would last before he'd start yelling for attention, she hugged the pillow to her cheek and just watched him entertaining himself.

Two minutes hadn't passed before her phone pinged softly with a motion alert and Stefan suddenly appeared in the frame.

She snatched up the phone. She didn't know what affected her more. The sight of him wearing just a pair of jeans or the sight of him entering Morgan's room.

"Hey, buddy," she heard him say softly while Morgan's bouncing slowed. He kept chewing the rail, but his eyes followed Stefan, who crouched near one corner of the crib. He held out his hand.

Justine realized he was holding out the plastic keys and even though neither baby nor man could see or hear her, she held her breath.

Morgan didn't take the keys though.

"We'll get there," Stefan said, finally reaching through the slats and setting the toy on the crib mattress. He straightened and lightly touched Morgan's hair before walking out of the monitor's view.

The creaking floorboards from the hallway faded quickly. Too quickly for Stefan to have headed to the stairs.

After a moment of looking around his new room and looking like he might cry, Morgan plopped down and snatched up the keys. He chewed on one. Made a pitiful sound.

She pulled on a knee-length sweater—it was the closest thing to a bathrobe that she owned—and cautiously pulled open her bedroom door.

Stefan's bedroom door at the end of the hallway was closed. Her heart beating too fast, she scurried into Morgan's room and closed his door with all the care of a thief.

"Mama!" Morgan abandoned the keys and reached out for her, his expression sunny once more.

He was the best tonic in the world.

She lifted him out of the crib and she changed his diaper, then sat down in the rocking chair to feed him.

Morgan grinned up at her as he nursed, and she couldn't help smiling back.

Then she heard the floorboards again and froze. In her mind's eye, she could picture Stefan creeping carefully past their rooms. When the creaking sped up, she knew he was closer to the head of the staircase.

She leaned down nearer to Morgan. "That's your father," she whispered. "Can you say daddy? How about d-d-d-dada?"

In response, he offered a gurgling smile of milk and kicking his foot against the arm of the rocking chair.

She tickled his chin and wiped his cheek with the sleeve of her sweater. "Pay attention to business there, bug. We've got a bath waiting for us both."

There was no denying that a full night of sleep

had done wonders. If she didn't let herself worry too much over Stefan, she felt almost as contented as Morgan.

By the time they'd splashed together in the huge tub, after which she'd dressed him in her favorite green-and-blue-plaid romper, she'd convinced herself that everything from here on out would be just fine.

The door to Stefan's bedroom was slightly ajar, revealing his bed.

Her curiosity took her two steps in that direction before she got control of herself.

She about-faced and went down the stairs like a drill sergeant was on her heels.

The coffee maker light was on, the coffeepot nearly full. A folded piece of paper with her name on the front sat tented on the counter.

She settled Morgan in his high chair with his plastic keys and his doughnut stacker and unfolded the note.

She hadn't seen Stefan's handwriting before. It wasn't quite illegible—as if his thoughts moved too fast to keep up—but it was close.

Have appts most of day. Call if you need.

It was a Tuesday morning. Of course, he had to work.

Was she surprised? Disappointed?

Relieved?

All three?

"Short and to the point." She showed the note to Morgan who tried to put it in his mouth.

She gave him a handful of cereal puffs instead.

Knowing that they were alone in the house, though, did have some advantages. She didn't feel like she was snooping around as she opened and closed cupboards and drawers, wanting to familiarize herself with the territory.

Almost all were empty except for one cupboard containing a clear plastic container of virulently orange cheese puffs.

"Orange." She let out a little laugh. "I might have known."

She closed the cupboard and turned to the boxes stacked against the wall. The two on top were from her apartment; the rest were sealed with packing tape. Obviously Stefan's.

The number of his boxes outweighed hers at least ten to one.

She fed Morgan and after spreading sunblock on him, tucked him in the carrier on her back and continued the exploring outside.

She aimed for the garden, surrounded by a rusty iron fence nearly obscured by overgrown plants.

At one point in time, some attempt at real gardening had been made. But the path through the large area was overgrown with weeds and the raised beds held nothing but shrunken and cracked soil. A plum tree was situated by itself in the center of the garden. A wooden garden bench sat disintegrating nearby.

She pulled one of the fruits off the tree and went back inside the house.

She washed the plum and took a bite. It was ripe and so juicy that it ran down her chin before she had a chance to stop it with a napkin. She peeled the rest and offered a small chunk to Morgan.

He gummed it and spat it out.

"You don't know what you're missing, bug."

She let him play on the floor with several plastic food containers, unpacked the rest of her stuff and started on Stefan's. He had a full set of china that she carefully washed in the sink and then she did a load of laundry and gathered the mail when she heard it drop through the mail slot on the front door.

Most of it was circulars. Only one envelope was actually addressed to Stefan. It was clearly a bill which reminded her to call the electric company to make sure the service at the apartment had been taken out of her name. The last item was a bridal magazine with no name on it at all.

She waved the magazine at the ceiling. "If this is you, Anika, cut it out." Then she put it in the trash only to take it right back out, because it wasn't *her* mail.

She stacked it—still sealed in its plastic—along with the circulars and the bill and left it all for him in the room that was supposed to be his study. It would look more like one if he had a proper desk instead of a bunch of boxes shoved together with a desk blotter placed on top.

She sent a group text message to her brothers with her new address and then she wandered around the house a while, imagining the parlor with a big fern in front of the window—the same as she'd grown up with. She sighed faintly and sent a text with her new address to her mom, too.

Her brothers all answered with various emojis.

Her mother didn't answer at all, but Justine could tell that Kimberly had read it.

Then Morgan was awake. She fed him and loaded him in the car, and they drove into town. She dropped off Gwen's house and apartment keys at the realtor's office. He wrote out a check, returning her overpaid rent.

She didn't know if he'd get it from the new owner or from Gwen, but when she deposited the money in her bank account, she decided it didn't really matter.

At the grocery store, she spent nearly half of what she'd deposited and could barely fit all the bags in her car. It seemed to take forever to cart them all into the house when they got back.

But at last it was done.

Stefan's china dishes were stored in Gwen's sideboard, a casserole was baking in the oven and Morgan was taking his afternoon nap upstairs when Stefan returned.

He took one step into the kitchen where she was sitting at the table with her laptop and stopped. "You unpacked all the boxes."

"It needed doing." Though he didn't look particularly pleased. She took off her reading glasses and set them on the table. "Is that a problem?"

"No." He shoved his fingers through his hair, leaving it standing up in wavy spikes. "I didn't think I'd be gone all day." He looked around. "What do I smell?"

"Chicken and rice casserole." Beneath his casual jacket, he wore a button-down shirt with the top two buttons undone. The image of him shirtless from the baby monitor that morning, however, was stuck in her head.

"Smells great. But just so you know, I don't expect you to cook."

She gave him a look. "Morgan and I have to eat, too."

He finally smiled. Ruefully. "Yeah." Then he pulled open the refrigerator door and whistled softly. "Did you leave anything on the shelves at the grocery store?"

"Not much."

She half expected him to make some comment about whether she'd used the credit card he'd given her and was grateful when he didn't. Instead, he just asked if Morgan was asleep.

She showed him the image on her phone from the baby monitor and turned her attention back to her computer. But all she could do was pretend to read. She was much too aware of him pulling out a bottle of beer before closing the refrigerator door.

He sat down in the chair across from her and twisted off the cap. "How'd it go today?"

Her gaze strayed to his arm. His wrist. His fingers when he spun the crimped bottle cap.

She militantly focused once more on her laptop. "Like usual. Just with more grocery bags. You?"

He let the bottle cap fall onto its side and pulled a piece of folded paper from his lapel pocket. He placed it on the table and slid it halfway across to her.

She put on her glasses again. The paper was thick, with an official feel. Even before she unfolded it and saw the name of the law firm at the top of the page, she knew what it would be.

"My lawyer advises an Agreed Paternity Order," he said.

Of course, the lawyer had. The court order did more than merely acknowledge paternity. It would specify Stefan's legal rights. Custody. Visitation. Child support. Medical support.

Prepared or not, reading the letter made something inside her clutch with panic.

Legally, Stefan's rights would be equal to hers.

What if they disagreed over something?

They were bound to at some point.

She was used to calling the shots when it came to Morgan. He was *her* baby.

"Don't think of this as protecting me or protecting you," Stefan said, as if he were reading her mind. "It protects Morgan."

Logically, she knew he was right. But emotionally?

"With you living here, at least visitation isn't an issue," he added in a clear attempt to lighten the mood.

"Child support shouldn't be either," she murmured, studying the amount that he was volunteering to pay. It was well above the required state percentage. "I could have afforded to stay in the apartment with this much financial support."

That very first day he'd said he was calling his lawyer to make sure Morgan was provided for. He'd obviously meant it. "Did you know about this before I found out about my rent?"

He didn't flinch. "Yes."

Her stomach hollowed a bit. "At least you're honest."

"You can have your own lawyer look over the terms."

"Like I *have* a lawyer."

"You can get one. I'll pay."

"The luxury of money," she murmured. She picked up the pen next to her laptop. One thing that she could say after spending the last six years of her life studying social work was that she understood the basics of family law. He was offering more than he needed to offer and asking no more than he deserved. Namely, joint custody.

She'd said she wasn't going to try to prevent Stefan from being Morgan's father, which meant that it was her responsibility to live up to her word, too.

She added her signature next to the little red sticker that said Sign Here, folded the paper and slid it back to him.

"Thank you."

Her nose prickled and she forced a smile. "So, what other trivial things did you do with your day?"

His smile looked as forced as hers. He returned the document to his jacket. "They started pouring the foundation for the brewery."

"That's fast, isn't it?"

"*Fast* is one of my specialties."

Despite everything, her mind went way too easily to a hotel suite in Florida. "Fast" had *not* been his way at all. Her skin heated even now thinking about the way he'd slowly driven her over the edge of insanity. Again. And again.

"Something wrong?"

His eyes saw too much. As if he knew exactly where her thoughts had gone.

Her phone vibrated once and she snatched it up, never more grateful in her life for the gift of the baby monitor. "Of course not." She flashed the screen at him that showed Morgan sitting up in his crib.

"Baby's awake," she said, and fled.

Chapter Ten

Aside from the momentousness of agreeing to the terms in the paternity order that Stefan's lawyer would file with the court, that first day set the tone for the ones that followed.

Stefan didn't always wait for Morgan to wake before going into his bedroom every morning. Sometimes he just went in for a few minutes and watched him sleep. One morning, he had a new toy to offer—a soft cloth book with pages that crinkled and jangled softly. It had a big orange giraffe on the front. Morgan hadn't wakened yet and Stefan silently left it in the crib.

By that afternoon, Morgan would hardly put the book down.

Stefan had attached the baby monitor to the wall the day after they'd gotten it, so he had to be aware that Justine might be witnessing his early-morning visits with their son.

But he didn't mention it, so neither did she.

When she and Morgan ventured downstairs each day, Stefan was already gone. He'd often send a text midday about some little thing or another and come home again in the late afternoon.

Instead of taking Morgan to a park, they spent hours outdoors right where they were. She bought a hard plastic baby pool and poured in a few bags of sand that she bought at the hardware store and plopped Morgan into the center of it.

The sides of the pool weren't tall enough to keep him contained if he really got it into his mind to escape, but with the sand and his toys, he was happy in the shade of the oak tree while she weeded and pinched back the leggy flowers near the front steps.

When she got tired of hauling around the leaky watering can that she'd found along with a bunch of other old tools in the spooky dark basement, they went back to the hardware store where she bought a hose and a pair of sturdy gardening gloves. Then she dragged the pool to the back and positioned it under the plum tree while she tried to beat the garden into some semblance of order with the rusty tools.

By the middle of the week, she'd finished cutting back some of the crazier branches of the plum tree and had a massive pile of trimmings from the overgrown shrubs that had obscured the iron fence.

Though Stefan didn't say much about her efforts—if anything she knew he would have told her they could hire someone to do the work—the trimmings were cleared away when she and Morgan returned from another trip to the grocery store. A bright new red wheelbarrow filled with equally new tools sat in the middle of the garden, along with several neatly stacked bags of fresh soil.

She'd sat on the stack and sniffled for ten minutes before getting herself back under control.

When a delivery truck arrived unexpectedly the next afternoon, she texted Stefan about it. He replied immediately.

Tell them to set it up in the study. We'll share.

She hadn't understood that last part until she realized what the delivery guys were setting up in the middle of the study was an old-fashioned partner's desk. Two-sided. Space for two people to face each other while they worked.

It had taken her a bit longer than ten minutes that time to recover. Particularly when the desk was followed by a wide, tall bookcase that would hold all of her textbooks and then some.

Her nose got pink from the sun; her arms and legs got tanned. And all the physical work helped exhaust her to the point that she slept at least a few hours at night without dreaming about the man who slept at the end of the hall.

She even managed to write her final term paper—sitting at a proper desk for the first time in nearly two years—and submitted it two days early and began working during Morgan's nap hours on her paying assignments.

"You're turning into a normal human being," Garland said in an email when Justine shared that detail. Garland was firmly Team Stefan and made no secret of it.

On Saturday afternoon following Morgan's nap, the three of them drove to Adam and Laurel's place.

Justine hadn't thought she was nervous until she saw what looked like a dozen vehicles parked near a house that bore a mild similarity to Stefan's.

He hesitated when her feet seemed to drag as they headed for the front door. "Don't tell me we've forgotten something." He was carrying the overstuffed baby backpack in one hand, in the other, a brimming striped beach bag she'd bought at the flea market. He was wearing a half-buttoned cotton shirt and board shorts and if it wasn't for the tray of homemade cookies he was juggling, he would have looked like he was heading to a day at the beach.

She, on the other hand, was just carrying Morgan and his bag of favorite toys. "We've got everything."

"Then what's wrong?"

She shifted Morgan to her other hip. It was probably her imagination, but it felt like he'd gained five pounds in the last week. "My social activities don't usually extend beyond coffee at Kirby's Perks."

She'd only gone once that week—neither Rebecca nor Annette had been there so early in the day and Bonita had given her the death stare as she'd prepared Justine's latte. If she hadn't witnessed Bonita preparing it, Justine would have been too afraid to drink it.

Stefan was watching her through narrowed eyes. "So?"

"I wouldn't be part of your—" her hands were too full to sketch air quotes, but her fingers tried anyway "—*group* here if it wasn't for you. I just—" She broke off and exhaled, unable to put into words what she meant.

"Are you trying to say you're shy?" He lifted his eyebrow. "Because you haven't had any problem with that where I'm concerned."

Her cheeks went even hotter. "Sure. Remind me of *that* right now."

He looked blank for a minute, then let out a bark of laughter. "Sweetheart, I just meant that you don't have a problem telling me what's on your mind. I wasn't talking about the way you propositioned me two minutes after we met."

"I did *not* proposition you two minutes after we met!" And if she'd told him everything that went through her head where he was concerned, he would have never thought the idea of them living platonically under the same roof had a lick of a chance.

"Okay, five minutes," he amended humorously.

"Relax. You were fine with my brothers and their wives." They'd reached the front door and before he could even lift his hand to knock, it was pulled open, and Laurel stood there.

"I saw you coming," she greeted with a wide smile. "We're all out back by the pool." She stepped aside long enough for them to enter the house. "Did you remember your swimsuit, Justine?"

"Unfortunately," she admitted. She hadn't worn it since Florida. "I haven't worn it since before I had Morgan."

Laurel laughed. "That's why we all love cover-ups. Are those homemade snickerdoodles?" She took the tray from Stefan and led them through the house.

"And thank-you for the baby monitor," Justine added. The furnishings were simple and welcoming and everywhere she looked glorious paintings hung on the walls. It made her postcard canvas hanging in her room seem childish. "It was a perfect gift."

"We've gone through three," Laurel admitted.

Given what Stefan had confided about Larkin, Justine wasn't surprised.

They walked through a sun-drenched great room where a gigantic wall-mounted television silently blasted cartoons, and out onto a covered patio over-looking a glittering pool. Three men, including Adam who was holding Larkin high in his arms, were already in the water. They were tossing a small basketball around.

Laurel set the cookies on a glass-topped table

amid a veritable feast of ice-chilled salads. "We're going cold today," she said, gesturing at the platter of fried chicken. "Too hot to grill out even with the pool. Stefan, do the honors and introduce Justine around, would you?"

Justine jumped a little when his hand touched the small of her back. His touch might be casual, but since he usually avoided contact altogether, it caused her no end of distraction.

"Adam's brothers," he said drawing her closer to the side of the pool. "Some of them, at least. You probably know Josh already." He didn't wait for her nod before addressing the man. "Where's your fiancée, Josh? She hasn't already come to her senses, has she?"

Kirby's youngest daughter was sitting on Josh's shoulders, and she squealed when he sent a stream of water splashing their way that Stefan managed to avoid with a quick sidestep. "If this wasn't a G-rated deal," Josh drawled, "I'd tell you what to do with yourself."

"Mommy had to work," Lily said. "Do the splash again!"

Josh obliged. This time, the water hit Stefan's legs but only because he couldn't back up without running into Lily's older sister, Violet.

"Kirby was set to come," Josh explained, "but she had to let an employee go."

Laurel looked up. "Surely not Hillary?"

"Bonita," Violet provided. "I didn't really like

her," she admitted before sitting on the edge of the pool and sticking her feet in the water.

"Neither did a lot of people," Josh added. He shrugged. "Bonita made great coffee but that doesn't work if she's flirting with one half of the customers and scaring off the other half."

Justine kept her agreement to herself and focused on the two boys on the far side of the pool. They were like two peas in a pod, both in looks and the way they cannonballed into the water. She'd seen them a few times at Kirby's Perks and knew they were Josh's nephews. "Toby and Tyler are sure growing."

"That's for sure," a striking redhead said, appearing just then with an infant in her arms. "Harper and Brady were just talking about that a few days ago."

Justine stared with surprise at her familiar face. "Emmaline!" She hadn't run into the antiques shop owner for months—not since she'd married Brian Fortune, soon after falling for the newest family member to arrive in town just after New Year's. "And this must be Allie," she crooned, admiring the baby. "She's beautiful." Justine looked from the baby to the third man in the pool. She'd only met Josh's brother once at Kirby's Perks and she felt a little dim now for not realizing they were Adam's brothers, too. "Brian?"

"Guilty," he answered despite the wild splashing of the boys who were trying to climb all over him.

"I guess introductions weren't necessary after all," Laurel said with a chuckle.

"Justine and I know each other from Kirby's Perks," Emmaline said.

"Yes," Justine admitted. "With my usual grace, I accidentally outed her pregnancy." In front of Brian, whom Emmaline had just been newly dating at the time. "How long ago was that? January?"

"Yes, which turned out fine," Emmaline said, giving her new husband a glance. Her expression was sublimely happy. "More than fine."

Justine found herself looking toward Stefan. But he was crouched next to the pool, feeling the water with his fingers, and didn't notice.

"Y'all, it's time to eat," Laurel called out to her guests. She plucked the edge of plastic wrap free from a bowl of potato salad as she gave Justine a rundown on the rest of Adam's siblings. "Kane and his wife are out of town. So's Arabella. She's in Red Rock with her husband. So we're a little light on Adam's family, but you know how it is trying to get everyone together in one place at one time."

"Takes a wedding or a funeral," Stefan said, then lifted his hands at the looks he earned. "What? I've got a big family, too. Don't pretend it isn't true."

"Yes, well," Laurel said, rolling her eyes a little. "Harper and the baby might be here later. But Brady's not going to make it. He has to work."

Justine had met Harper, too. She'd helped arrange the small baby shower at Kirby's Perks for Emmaline. She also knew Harper's husband, Brady Fortune, was the concierge at the Hotel Fortune and was

Brian's twin. "I never connected the dots between all of you and Stefan's business partner," she admitted and caught the quick look that passed between Laurel and Emmaline.

She could just imagine what they were thinking.

Not even two weeks ago, Justine had been just another single mom with an addiction to coffee at Kirby's Perks. There'd been no dots to connect between her and Stefan, either, because she'd never spoken about him.

And now here she was, living with him.

No matter how welcoming they were, Justine could sense the questions they wanted to ask. But didn't.

Instead they got situated around the big patio table. There was so much chatter and food passing around that she finally stopped worrying about what anyone else was speculating where she and Stefan were concerned.

Before long, talk turned to the double *B*s. Brewery and babies. Food and cookies were demolished. Emmaline took Allie inside to put her down for a nap, and Justine took Morgan inside to change his diaper and give herself a pep talk about swimsuits. Emmaline was wearing one and she'd become a mom only a few months ago.

Justine used one of the bedrooms to change. No matter how much she adjusted the top of her tankini, there was no pretending her bustline wasn't considerably more generous than it had been the last time she'd worn it. She had to settle for pulling the top of it as high as it would go to keep her cleavage from popping out all over. She didn't have a stylishly colorful sarong like Emmaline, though she did have a beach towel.

But it was a choice of either covering her top or covering her hips and thighs. She wrapped it around her waist, picked up Morgan again and left the room.

Brian's nephews and Kirby's daughters were clustered in front of the oversize television watching a Disney show. None of them even glanced her direction as she passed them on her way back out to the patio.

"There she is," Stefan said as soon as she showed her face. "She can tell you."

"Tell you what?" She turned away and made a project of closing the sliding French door behind her. She was certain it was her imagination that Stefan's gaze had lingered on her chest, but her nipples had pebbled anyway.

"About Chatelaine," Josh said. "Stefan says you grew up there."

"Yes." While she'd been inside, a portable fenced enclosure had been set up in the shady grass to contain Larkin away from the pool. "Can I—"

"Oh, yeah," Adam assured and without a blink lifted Morgan out of Justine's arms and set him down inside the space with Larkin. It happened so fast that Morgan didn't have a chance to protest and then he was faced with Larkin who fascinated him as much as ever.

Stefan's expression was unreadable as he upended

the bag of toys in with him. Morgan snatched up his giraffe and offered it to Larkin along with a stream of gibberish while Stefan pulled his shirt over his head and did a shallow dive into the pool. He executed it so cleanly, the water barely rippled.

Feeling bemused, Justine returned to her seat. She watched Stefan stretch out beneath the surface of the water as he swam. He didn't come up for air until he reached the far end of the pool. "What about Chatelaine?" she asked absently.

"Belle—do you know Belle?" Josh didn't wait for her to answer which was good because she was totally distracted by Stefan slicking back his water-black hair with one flick. "She's our cousin. Has it in her head that the solution to our little mystery can be found in Chatelaine."

She finally managed to look away from Stefan. "Nothing interesting ever happens in Chatelaine."

"Remember the Alonzo Flynn statue I told you about? The ugly horse head," Emmaline prompted, "that was given anonymously to Brady—"

"—who dumped it in *my* lap," Brian inserted. "So he didn't have to deal with the hideous thing on his honeymoon." He grinned. "Typical brother."

"Speak for yourself," Adam said lazily. He was toying with the ends of Laurel's hair as he kept an eye on the kid corral.

"I remember." Justine looked at Emmaline but from the corner of her eye she saw Stefan brace his arms on the side of the pool and pull himself out, all gleaming muscle, sinew and streaming water. She swiped at her hair, pushing it back from her suddenly damp forehead. "You found a key in the base of it."

Emmaline nodded. "A key that opened a safe deposit box at a bank in Austin."

Brian kissed her knuckles. "The city where you made an honest man out of me."

The adoration between the two was palpable.

Justine didn't want to say she was envious. But she did reach blindly for the last snickerdoodle and shove it into her mouth. Stefan had picked up a towel and he flipped it around his neck as he pulled a beer bottle from an oval tub filled with melting ice. He twisted off the cap and took a long drink.

Perfectly G-rated.

Unless your name was Justine Maloney.

She grabbed for her own glass of water and barely managed not to knock it over.

"Long story not so short—" she realized that Josh had taken over the tale again. "The safe deposit box contained a poem that made as little sense as everything else. About mines, but none of us made *that* connection until I received the travel book on Texas last month."

She remembered the conversation she'd overheard between Stefan and his brothers the day they'd moved her out of her apartment. Remembered too the evening not long before that when Josh and Kirby had celebrated their engagement at Kirby's Perks. It was there that Justine had first seen Mark Mendoza.

A few days later, Stefan showed up and turned her world inside out.

Again.

She didn't dare look in his direction. "That's the book you mentioned when you and Kirby were celebrating your engagement at the coffee shop?" Not only had Mark startled her, but so had hearing the name of her own hometown.

Josh nodded. "Showed up as mysteriously as Brian's horse."

"I still think you're looking for shadows that aren't there." Stefan ambled back to the table. "Stuff gets misdelivered all the time. Don't see me conjecturing the mysteries of a bridal magazine that came in the mail the other day."

She cursed the heat that filled her face as if *she'd* been the one to send it to him.

She was the one who'd *refused* marrying him.

Now she wished she'd left the thing in the trash.

"I'd agree with you," Josh was saying, "but even though the clues haven't been very clear, they're obviously meant to lead us somewhere." He held up his fingers, ticking them off. "Belle received that framed picture of a rose when she got to town in December. At the time she just thought it was some standard welcome to Rambling Rose."

"But it had an inscription on the back." Emmaline picked up the story. "'A rose, by any other name would smell as sweet.' Followed by the initials MAF."

Stefan pulled out his chair and sat. He swiped one end of his towel absently down his chest.

Justine's eyeballs felt blistered.

Josh ticked off another finger. "Mariana heard the calypso record that Draper received and remembered her mom singing one of the songs when she was a little girl."

Emmaline leaned sideways toward Justine. "That's what prompted Mariana to get the DNA test. Well, that plus a pink blanket with a monogrammed *F* that was shipped to Beau a couple of months ago." She must have read Justine's confusion. "Draper and Beau are Belle's brothers."

Laurel sat forward. "I was at Provisions the day Mariana recognized her mother as a child in one of the old prints hanging on the wall. She was with several children in front of the Foundling Hospital."

Justine knew that the Foundling Hospital had once stood at the site of the pediatric center.

"Mariana's mother was the only one with a blanket and it had a monogrammed F in the corner, too," Laurel continued. "She never knew that her mother had been adopted, you see. But ever since she saw the photo—what? Two years ago?" She looked toward her husband, who nodded. "She says she's been wondering about it. Then Beau gets the same kind of blanket that her mother had, something like eighty years earlier?"

Justine glanced at Stefan. Still shirtless. Still soaking wet, water droplets gleaming on his rock-hard abs and muscular thighs. Even as interesting as it was to get this close a glimpse into what had mostly been just coffee-shop gossip to her over the past several months, it was hard to get too interested when most of her senses were hitting overload because of him.

He was tossing toys back into the kiddie corral, making Morgan chortle as he crawled after them.

Stefan's slow-but-steady approach where Morgan was concerned was finally paying off.

"Obviously, whoever is sending the gifts now is near enough when they're received to be aware of the results," Brian said. "Why else would I have received that letter at Em's shop the way I did?"

Emmaline again interpreted for Justine's benefit. "The letter gave Brian access to use the key from the horse statue at the bank in Austin."

"Who sent it?" Justine managed to drag her attention back to the conversation at hand. "The bank or the person who owned the safe deposit box?"

Both Emmaline and Brian shook their heads.

"It wasn't the bank," Brian said, "not that ruling them out helped answer anything. When we went back to use the key, they still wouldn't say who owned the box. But my name was on record there, giving me access all the same."

"You forgot the best part," Emmaline prompted. "In the envelope with the letter was a slip of paper." She waved her palm in the air like she was declaring a headline. "'The Key to the Future.'" She dropped her hand and shrugged. "That's all it said, but clearly it was a reference to the safe deposit key."

"So, what was actually *in* the box?" Justine asked. "Information about Mariana's parents?" Was Mariana supposed to be MAF or one of her parents?

Being enthralled by Stefan wasn't helping her keep up with things.

"Only thing in the box was a poem," Josh said, taking up the story again. "However, that brings me back to the book *I* received."

"Are we all talking about that book *again*?" a cheerful voice complained from behind them.

They all looked around to see Kirby coming out the French doors. She squeezed Justine's shoulder on her way around the table to kiss her fiancé, who promptly pulled her down onto his lap.

"I passed the kids on my way through," she said with a laugh. "*All* asleep. Even Violet."

"Didn't think you were going to make it," Josh said to her.

"Hillary offered to finish off the day. She knew we'd had plans. And for a Saturday, it was pretty slow." Kirby's smile turned rueful. "The ice cream shop, though, had a line out the door."

Laurel offered to get a clean plate, but Kirby waved it off. "Just tell me. Have we learned something new in the Mariana mystery?"

Josh shook his head. "I was just talking about the line in the safe-deposit poem that mentioned mines.

And the highlighted page in the book that talks about the silver mines near Chatelaine."

Justine suddenly felt at the center of everyone's attention.

Even Stefan's.

She lifted her shoulders, which messed with her carefully adjusted swimsuit that immediately slipped right down to its usual spot. Cleavage and all. "I know there are abandoned mines around Chatelaine. I just don't know anything about their history. But," she added quickly at their falling expressions, "there is a museum. It has a whole section devoted to mining. Used to, anyway."

"Booyah." Josh sat back, looking satisfied.

She wasn't sure why. She doubted the museum had changed a lick since she and her sixth-grade elementary class had been forced to tour it. "What exactly did the poem say?"

Emmaline began reciting.

"'What is mine is yours. What is yours is mines.

I hope you can read between the lines.

Love is forever; love never dies.

You'll see it too, when you look in her eyes.'"

"It was signed with the same MAF initials as Belle's rose print," Brian finished. "No question everything's connected."

"Connected to Mariana Fortune," Adam said to no one in particular. "Mystery solved."

"Spoilsport," Laurel chided lightly. "What if the

answer to Mariana's parents is just a couple hours away?"

"Everyone kind of knows everyone in Chatelaine," Justine said. "The only time I ever heard of anyone named Fortune, it was because they were in the news for one reason or another." Hosting galas or advertising blue jeans or getting arrested for arson and kidnapping. When it came to the name, the stories ran the gamut.

She suddenly couldn't help looking around the table with her own dose of speculation.

"All I know is that Belle's whipped up over going to Chatelaine," Josh told Justine before giving Stefan a decidedly amused look. "She's like a dog with a bone when she sets her mind to something."

Stefan's lips twisted. He seemed to be studying the bottle he'd propped on his hard abdomen.

Josh looked back at Justine. "Should I tell her you might be willing to play tour guide? Worst you'll get out of it is an afternoon of her *endless* energy."

"We could drive separately," Stefan suggested.

"You'd want to go?" Justine's mouth tasted a little sour. Was he interested just because of Belle?

He nodded. "It'll give me a chance to meet your mom."

"She's on vacation," she lied abruptly. "And I'm not even sure the museum's open during the summer," she warned, hoping to get away from the topic of her mother.

"It is." Adam looked up from his phone. "According to the website I just found. But only on Wednesdays and Saturdays."

"If it's Saturday you're talking, we're out," Emmaline said. "I'm running a sale at my shop and Brian's promised to help."

"Hillary has the coffee shop covered next weekend so you could leave Morgan with us," Kirby offered. "You know the girls adore him. And vice versa. I'm sure he'd be fine with us for the day as long as he'll take a bottle."

That much was true.

And Justine did have plenty of frozen breast milk.

"What do you say, Justine?" Josh coaxed. "An afternoon in Chatelaine?"

Her gaze collided with Stefan's.

She wanted badly to get out of the entire situation. Not because she wasn't curious about Mariana's connection to Chatelaine or because she didn't want to leave Morgan in Kirby's capable hands. Or even because she didn't want Stefan to find out about her mother's attitude toward their son.

Purely and simply, it meant spending even more time with *him* and she wasn't sure how much more she could take. Especially when she wondered if Belle's involvement was the real lure for him.

He was still looking at her.

She smiled weakly. "Chatelaine, it is."

Chapter Eleven

By the next Saturday, the troop of people heading to Chatelaine had expanded to not only include Belle and her brothers Beau and Draper, but Mark and Rodrigo as well.

Mariana had chosen to stay behind.

"I can't stand the stress," she'd said when Stefan saw her earlier that week at Roja. "Y'all can tell me what you find out."

Even without Mariana, the procession from Rambling Rose to Chatelaine involved several vehicles.

And the closer they got to Justine's hometown, the quieter she became.

Stefan was certain she'd lied about her mother being away. He just didn't know why.

"Worried about Morgan?" he asked as they drove past the city limit sign which marked nothing at all but a lot of dried grass lining the highway and a run-down house way off in the distance.

She made a soft sound and shook her head. She was wearing the same paisley dress with the stretchy top she'd worn the first day he'd gone to her apartment, along with bright pink sneakers, and she kept pleating the fabric over her thighs between her fingertips.

"It does feel strange without him though," she offered eventually. She looked over her shoulder at the empty backseat.

Even though everyone else had doubled up in vehicles, she and Stefan were the only ones in his truck.

She faced forward again. "It was nice of you to drive."

"You weren't likely to invite me otherwise."

She gave him a quick look. "That's not true."

"Isn't it?"

She pressed her lips together.

"When it comes to the purpose of this escapade, I'm along for the ride just as much as you are," she finally said.

Which told him nothing more than he already knew. That she accepted his presence in her life because of Morgan.

He drummed his thumb against the steering wheel. She'd been living with him for nearly two weeks now. Except for his own bedroom, there was hardly a space where she hadn't left her mark.

He felt like he was balancing on the sharp side of a double-edged sword.

She watched the gas station they passed where a single lonely pump stood in the front. "Welcome to Chatelaine. The town that never changes. Harv's New BBQ straight ahead."

The restaurant was the location where Belle had suggested they all meet before proceeding to the museum.

Even though his truck was in the lead, it was Belle Fortune who'd planned it all. Soon as she'd discovered that Justine was on board, she'd set about organizing the day with the thoroughness of a general going to battle.

Harv's had a big sign on the side of the road and the parking lot was packed when Stefan turned into it.

When the rest of their convoy turned in, every spot was filled.

Justine pushed open her door and slid out as soon as Stefan turned off the engine.

He sighed faintly and followed.

He'd barely made any inroads where Morgan was concerned. And sometimes it felt like he was losing ground where Justine was concerned.

Belle, typically, ordered everyone around as soon as her feet hit the gravel of the parking lot.

"It's a beautiful day," she said brightly. "Let's sit at the tables outside."

Finally, Justine gave Stefan a faint smile. "There aren't any tables *inside*," she said under her breath.

Everyone ordered individually at the counter and carried their food out to the plain wood tables that surrounded the building and munched on pulled pork and brisket sandwiches and house-made kettle chips.

"Nothing orange," Stefan observed.

Justine laughed and he felt like he'd won a prize.

After lunch, they loaded up the vehicles again, only this time Belle announced that she would ride with Stefan and Justine.

He ignored the looks his brothers gave him and hoped that Justine didn't notice them, either.

For a brief time at the beginning of the year, Belle had set her sights on Stefan despite his very intentional effort to discourage her. Fortunately, he'd escaped those sights when she'd fallen in love with Jack Radcliffe.

Stefan had been so relieved he'd sent the newly engaged couple an entire case of wine.

"I talked to the docent at the museum," Belle said as they drove the short block and pulled into another parking lot. Her engagement ring winked in the sunshine as she leaned over their seat and showed off her notes. "She's supposed to be working this afternoon. Name's Connie."

Justine stirred. "Connie Rios?"

"Yes. Do you know her?"

Justine nodded.

"Even better."

Stefan parked and they all got out. Belle trotted over to her brothers, presumably to share the news that Justine knew Connie Rios.

It hardly seemed exciting to him, but then he hadn't come on this snipe hunt to solve any mysteries besides the mystery of the woman living with him.

Belle was in fine form, bustling Justine to the head of their line as they entered the museum.

From the outside, the building looked more like a white adobe house with a red-tiled roof. On the inside though, it was cool and hushed, with aged wood floors and photos hung gallery-style on every wall.

The bell over the door was still ringing when a petite woman appeared. She was even shorter than Belle, with a thick ponytail and a wide smile that got wider when she spotted Justine. "As I live and breathe!" She held out her arms. "Justine Maloney. I thought you'd dropped clean off the edge of the earth!"

Justine looked rueful as she submitted to the hug. "You haven't charged at all, Connie." When she straightened, she introduced everyone. "If there's any history in this town, Connie knows it back and forward. She's been volunteering at the museum since we were in high school."

"And I actually receive a salary now," Connie said humorously.

"We're hoping to find some history regarding a

woman named Mariana Sanchez," Belle said, getting right down to business. "Her mother's name was Maribel Sanchez. We're thinking that Maribel might have been born here, but somehow ended up in the Foundling Hospital in Rambling Rose."

"Sanchez?" Connie mused. "Not an unusual name around here. Has Ms. Sanchez checked with the department of vital statistics?"

"They didn't turn up anything, either."

"How long ago would her mother have been born?"

"We're not sure exactly. Maybe eighty to eighty-five years ago." Belle glanced around at the rest of them, seeming to want their corroboration before she continued. "She might have been connected to someone with the initials MAF or even named Fortune, but Mariana isn't entirely certain about that either. The initials could be referring to *her*, just as easily as her mother. Chatelaine's population back then had to have been pretty small, wouldn't it?"

"Not necessarily. Ranching's the mainstay. Always has been. For a while, though, prospectors came from all over, hoping to make their fortunes." Connie pursed her lips for a moment, then led them from the main room and down a hall.

Following along, Stefan realized the museum was larger than it appeared from the front. There were rooms devoted to the first settlers of Chatelaine, the early farmers, early politicians, early everything.

There wasn't space for all of them in the office

that Connie turned into, and he was content to hang to the back. He could still hear her talking about the town's project to digitize its public records. "There's still nothing quite like poring through dusty old ledgers," Connie was saying as computer keys clacked. "Maribel, you say?"

Stefan wandered along the hallway. On one side were more photos. On the other was an enormous map—nothing but lines and handwritten street names in a neat but fading cursive.

He heard footsteps and knew without looking that they were Justine's.

"That was my elementary school." She pointed to a picture of a small square building. "My favorite place was the playground."

He smiled, imagining her with pigtails and skinned knees. "And high school? What was your favorite place there? The library?"

Her lips curved ruefully. "Shows, does it?"

"In the best way."

Her gaze flicked to his, then away again.

He turned to look at the map. "Where'd you live?"

Her hesitation was barely noticeable before she moved next to him. She tapped two intersecting lines and turned back toward Connie's office where Belle and the others were just leaving.

"When you think about it," Connie was saying, "it's not surprising that I can't find mention of either Maribel or her daughter. A lot of the children who ended up at the foundling hospital were either orphans or illegitimate. Considering the number of prospectors who came through here—all the way up to the 1950s actually—illegitimate births were more frequent than people like to admit. Everyone knew it was happening, but polite society still considered it scandalous, so families worked hard to keep it under wraps. Birth records should have been registered in the locale they occurred, but money was passing hands all the time for one thing or another."

"Sounds right up a Fortune's alley," Beau murmured.

Belle hushed him. "They haven't all been rapscallions."

"Haven't they?"

Belle glared at him. "I hate going back empty-handed."

"What were they prospecting?" Stefan asked Connie.

"Silver mostly. Copper. Gold was rarely found and usually as a result of the silver mining." Connie reached for a handful of colorful brochures. "We had these done up a few years ago for our centennial celebration." She handed them out. "The mines were abandoned long ago but people still like to seek them out. Good day hikes, usually. Most of them have little gift shops and such still operating. Even the ones without official tour guides. If nothing else, you can get a cold drink. Sometimes even a piece of homemade fudge."

"Let's split up," Belle suggested.

"For what?" Draper asked. "You think we're going to find something laying in the dirt outside an abandoned mine?"

Belle gave her brother a cool stare and opened the brochure to the map. "Can we reach these easily still this afternoon?" she asked Connie. "It's already past noon."

"Don't see why not." Connie circled an area with a highlighter pen. "This is roughly a ten-mile radius. If you wanted to visit more than one before dark, you could manage it."

Belle divvied up the mines and they all left to head off in opposite directions.

The silver mine assigned to Stefan and Justine happened to not only have the requisite gift shop, but a large hand-painted sign proclaiming Tour Mine Here!

While Justine wandered through the little shop that was crowded with everything from kids' slingshots to hand-painted scarves and jewelry, Stefan paid the modest fee for the tour to an old bearded guy sitting in one corner on a wood barrel.

"Starts in ten minutes," the old man said. "Sharp."

Stefan glanced around the gift shop. Aside from an equally old woman, he and Justine were the only other people around.

"We'll be here," he assured, and went over to Justine where she was standing in front of a jewelry case guarded by the eagle-eyed woman. She had a sticker on her bosom that said her name was Geraldine.

Justine was toying with a delicately coiled silver bracelet with a shining blue stone in the center.

"That's moonstone," Geraldine said. "And silver from right here at the Joyride. Try it on."

Justine slipped the bracelet on her wrist. "How much is it?"

The woman told her, and Justine laughed softly and slipped it right back off her wrist. She handed it back and adjusted the strap of her macramé purse hanging crosswise over her shoulders. "It's beautiful but way out of my budget."

Geraldine had wild gray hair, a million wrinkles and a missing tooth that showed when she let out a rusty laugh. "That's what they all say." She placed the bracelet back in the glass case.

At ten minutes, *sharp*, Stefan and Justine stopped in front of the bearded guy, who donned a miner's helmet complete with a light on the front and shuffled off his stool.

"I'm Harv," he boomed suddenly, as if he was addressing a crowd of two hundred, "and I'll be your tour guide today."

Justine's eyes flew to Stefan's. They were filled with more mirth than they'd held all day.

"Any relation to Harv's barbecue?" Stefan asked.

"My good fer nothin' grandson," Harv said, and pushed at the primitive wood wall behind him.

It slid back to reveal a wide set of shallow steps carved into the ground. "Watch yer step now," he said, descending the stairs with surprising speed.

"This here's the Joyride Silver Mine, established in 1894."

Despite his skepticism, Stefan was soon as engrossed as Justine seemed to be by the old man's vivid depictions of life for those people who came hoping to strike it rich.

"Some succeeded," Harv said, sucking at his teeth and turning down yet another underground tunnel bolstered by thick beams of wood that looked as old as time itself. "Most didn't. There was avarice working alongside charity. Corruption versus virtue. We had it all and then some."

Stefan ducked his head to avoid a low-hanging lantern. "How long was the mine active?"

"Finally tapped out in 1937." Harv started leading the way back through the maze. They'd walked more than two miles, start to finish with Harv pointing out the distances marked in the hard-packed walls. "My granddad and my pa both worked it. Gramps was old. Pop was young. Didn't earn 'em nothing but a halfway honest wage, but in all that time, the mine still yielded more 'n ten million dollars. Be a helluva lot more in today's currency." He grinned. "Lot of folks don't think mining when they think of Texas, but that don't mean it weren't happening." He pushed past them and went back up the steps. "Fortunes were being made and lost every day."

"Wonder if Maribel Sanchez was one of those lost Fortunes," Justine whispered as they reached the doorway and Harv pushed the wood back in place, hiding the mine entrance once again.

"Don't see how we'll ever know." Stefan still considered that particular hunt a waste of time. But the way that Justine was smiling at him had been worth every minute.

Justine shook Harv's hand warmly. "You're a wonderful storyteller, Harv."

The old man colored above the gnarly beard. "Ah, go on, now."

Justine laughed and glanced around. "Restroom?"

"Out back of the gift shop," Geraldine provided as she offered Harv a cup of something that looked— and smelled—suspiciously like whiskey.

"Won't be long," Justine said and skipped out of the shop, her purse flopping against her hip.

Stefan gave Harv a generous tip for the tour and returned to the glass case and the coiled bracelet. "Can you wrap that up before she gets back?"

"Faster than you can pull out a credit card," Geraldine said with a wink.

He smiled and pulled out his wallet.

The box containing the bracelet was buried in his truck's glove compartment and he was waiting outside the gift shop with a couple bottles of water and a plain paper sack of old-fashioned candy sticks when Justine reappeared.

He pulled two sticks from the bag. "Root beer or grape?"

"I used to love these things." She took the root

beer and peeled back one end of the plastic wrap. She sucked the end of the candy and Stefan suddenly questioned the wisdom of his choice.

He cleared his throat and focused on his own candy but the image of Justine savoring hers was stuck hard in his head.

"Geraldine gave me another map," he said. "Walking tour if you're interested. Supposed to end up at a lake."

Justine slipped the candy stick to the corner of her mouth. "Sure." She seemed in no hurry to end the afternoon just yet. "One of those bottles for me?"

He gave it to her, and they set off, her in the lead as she followed the roughly marked path. The lake, when they reached it, wasn't much more than a pond. But it was pretty and shaded and they sat together on the grassy bank, sucking on hard candy and sipping water.

"You never knew this was here?"

She shook her head and leaned back until she was prone, her knees bent beneath the paisley dress. She shielded her eyes with her arm as she stared up at the deeply blue sky. "Never knew. If my brothers did, they never mentioned it."

Stefan lay back, too. But the sky held considerably less interest to him. He propped his head on his hand and studied her, instead. "Was it hard for you? Being pregnant and alone in Chatelaine?"

She gave him a startled look. "Being in Chatelaine

was hard," she admitted after a while. "But the only one worried about a scandal was my mother."

"Is that why you don't want to go by and see her?"

Her caramel-colored gaze flickered. "I told you. She's on vacation."

He drew his finger down her warm forearm. It was a poor substitute for finding out if her kiss would taste of root beer candy, but it was a heck of a lot smarter.

She huffed slightly and crunched the last remaining sliver of her candy stick. "Trust me," she muttered. "She doesn't want to see me, either."

It didn't take a genius to recognize that she wasn't happy about her admission. Even though he was glad she'd been honest, he was a lot less happy that he'd been the cause of it. "I'm sorry."

"You don't have to be sorry. Regardless of what she thinks, Morgan's the best thing that ever happened to me." She sat up suddenly and rolled to her feet, rubbing her arm where he'd touched her. "We should probably be getting back."

He stood as well. He'd pushed too hard, too fast. But it still felt like the wall between them had one less brick.

She was silent as they drove back to Rambling Rose. They'd just reached the town limits when Stefan's cell phone rang. It was his father telling him that he'd be in Rambling Rose in a week. "Can't wait to meet my grandson!" Esteban's voice was as booming over the Bluetooth connection as Harv's. "Not to mention his mama."

When he rang off, Justine wore a faint smile. "At least Morgan has one grandparent who's excited to see him."

Stefan reached over and squeezed her hand.

The fact that she didn't pull away meant the world.

Chapter Twelve

Even though Justine hadn't worried—much—about Morgan being in Kirby's care, she was still grateful to pick him up.

"His feet never touched the ground thanks to the girls wanting to carry him all day," Kirby said ruefully as she packed up Morgan's toys that had been scattered around. "He had two short naps and was fine with the bottle feeding. Maybe because Violet insisted on being the one to offer it to him."

"I appreciate you watching him," Justine said. Talking about bottle feeding only reminded her how much she needed to nurse. And Morgan knew it, too, judging by the way he started fussing and pulling at the neckline of her dress.

"It was our pleasure. So, did you solve any mysteries in Chatelaine?"

Not about Mariana, Justine thought. But at least she was able to put to rest the notion that Stefan had been interested in Belle Fortune.

She knew what attraction looked like in Stefan's face and he'd shown absolutely none when they'd been together.

Instead, he'd looked at Justine as if he'd wanted to kiss her as much as she'd wanted him to.

"Not about the mines," she finally answered Kirby. Even the others had reported interesting enough hikes but nothing that seemed relevant.

Kirby's eyes searched Justine's face. "Did you have a good *time* at least?" She waited a beat. "With Stefan?"

Justine felt her face flush and focused on Morgan. "It was…interesting," she allowed and dragged her dress back above her bra line.

Kirby immediately recognized the situation. "Go," she said. "We can catch up next time. Latte will be on the house." She followed Justine out to the truck and waved at Stefan while Justine quickly fastened Morgan into his car seat. It wasn't easy with him fussing.

"I can't believe I forgot to tell you." Kirby opened the passenger door for her when Justine straightened. "Martin's been transferred to a rehab center."

She was so stunned she momentarily forgot about her throbbing breasts. "He's doing *better*?"

"Miraculously." Kirby gave her a quick kiss on her cheek and stepped back while Justine climbed inside the truck. "The only reason they didn't send him directly home from the hospital is because they're concerned about him living alone." She pushed the door shut and stepped back, waving.

Stefan pulled away from the curb. "Who's Martin?"

"One of the Kirby's Perks regulars. He's been in the hospital." She winced as she buckled her seat belt.

"What's wrong?"

"Nothing." She waved her hands toward the windshield just as Morgan started wailing. "Let's just go."

She could hear Stefan's muttered oath.

"He'll calm down as soon as we get home and I can nurse him," she defended. One portion of her mind realized that she'd used the word *home* for the first time. The rest of her was consumed by the sound of her baby crying.

It was *not* helping her situation at all.

Instead of speeding up, though, Stefan was pulling over to the curb.

"What are you doing?"

He shoved the truck into Park, got out and opened the back door. He freed Morgan from the car seat, yanked open Justine's door and plopped the baby into her arms. "Feed him. You have breasts. They make milk. So do what nature intends and stop worrying that I might see a nipple or two in the process."

Her cheeks burned, but her milk was already

starting to leak, and she hastily dragged aside her bra to let Morgan nurse. "I wasn't the one worrying about it," she said hotly even as relief drained through her when Morgan latched. "You're the one who always takes a hike or looks relieved when I leave the room to nurse him." She yanked the door shut again, leaving him standing there on the sidewalk.

She leaned her head back against the seat and closed her eyes.

Stefan climbed back behind the steering wheel. "I didn't mean to make you feel like you had to nurse him in private. I thought *you* wanted it that way."

She didn't open her eyes. "Maybe I did. Some."

"He sounds like he's gulping," he said after a long while.

"He is. He's hungry."

"We stayed out too long."

She finally opened her eyes.

Stefan looked as discontented as Morgan looked contented.

She switched him to her other breast, deftly unfastening and refastening the cups of her nursing bra within mere seconds. "We didn't stay out too long. I should've just taken time to nurse him at Kirby's. I didn't expect him to start crying like that."

"Probably afraid I was going to touch him," Stefan muttered. "Which I did."

His hand was clenched on the console between their seats.

"Give me your hand."

He gave her a suspicious look that was uncannily similar to those that Morgan often gave him. "Why?"

"I know where Morgan gets it," she murmured. "Just give me your hand."

He relaxed his fist and lifted his hand. She took it and cupped it around the back of Morgan's dark, curly hair.

The baby didn't stop suckling. His eyes were wide as he looked up at the two of them.

It wasn't quite dark yet. She could see the way Stefan's gaze flickered. He couldn't seem to tear his eyes away from his son.

She rested her head against the backrest once more and closed her burning eyes.

There didn't seem to be a single thing she could do to stop herself from falling for her son's daddy.

While he, on the other hand, was only falling for their son.

Morgan was finished eating in a matter of ten minutes, but in that small amount of time, evening had fallen.

Justine's breasts felt blessedly empty for the first time since that morning even though she'd pumped and dumped a couple of times throughout the day. Her bodice adjusted, she fastened Morgan into his car seat, and they drove the rest of the way home.

Home. There was that word again.

Stefan parked near the front porch. She carried Morgan inside and Stefan followed with the baby bag. "I'm going to give him his bath," she said, walking through the dark house while he flipped on the lights. She hesitated when they reached the base of the stairs. "D'you want to help?"

His smile was slow. "Thank you."

She'd fallen for that smile at a New Year's Eve party nearly eighteen months ago. Falling for it again was much, much too dangerous.

She forced herself to look away and start up the steps. "Have you already forgotten how he likes to splash?"

"Nope." Stefan's chuckle followed her, curling like an embrace around her nerves. "I'll survive," he said.

He would.

Would she?

She admitted as much two days later when Garland called. Her jet-setting friend was back in Chicago again, placing them within the same time zone for once.

"What's so bad about falling for Stefan?" Garland asked. "He's successful. He's willing to pay you more child support than he's required, plus keep a roof over your head. Do you know how many fathers weasel out of doing either one of those things?"

Justine *did* know.

Morgan was in his improvised sandbox in a patch of shade and Justine paced around the garden. She'd transplanted a variety of flowers in the refreshed raised beds and, so far, they were flourishing. Hard for them not to, considering how much time she spent out there fussing with them in her attempts to keep her hands and mind off Stefan.

"The only reason I'm here is because it's the most expedient way for him to have Morgan here," she said again. "He's not in love with me."

"Are *you* in love with him?" Garland asked swiftly.

"Of course not." Even as she said the words, she knew they were a lie.

Garland probably knew, too, but she had the kindness not to point it out.

"Anyway," Garland said, "I gotta go, but I called my mom for that recipe you wanted for plum jam. I'll email it to you soon as we hang up."

"Thanks." Justine clapped her hands loudly, scattering the birds that were trying to make a feast on the fruit. She had plans for that fruit.

Not just jam. But with Stefan's father coming, she'd decided to make her mom's blackberry-plum tart. She was nervous enough about meeting him. She didn't dare attempt making something that wasn't familiar.

"And call me after Stefan's dad visits," Garland ordered. "I want to know how the big night goes. Still can't believe you offered to cook for him and Stefan's brothers, too."

"Neither can I," she muttered, but Garland had already hung up.

Justine pocketed her phone and clapped her hands again.

Wings flapped all over again and Morgan laughed so hard he started hiccupping.

Even though Justine had plans, she waited for the birds to return, just to do it all over again.

Plums were one thing.

Days of sunshine and baby laughter were another.

Eventually, though, it was time to go inside.

Morgan had so much sand in his clothes she stripped them off altogether and carried him inside wearing just his diaper.

The sight of Stefan and Josh inside the kitchen made her stop short. She hadn't expected Stefan, much less someone else, until later that afternoon. After she'd had a chance to shower.

Stefan didn't seem to notice anything about her at all, though, as he waved her over. "Josh wants to finish up the new renovation plans."

Kirby's fiancé was moving around the kitchen with a tape measure in his hand. "Your original idea was to pull out all the original cabinets. Are you *sure* you don't want to replace them?" he asked.

"No," Stefan said.

"Yes," Justine said at the same time.

Stefan smiled ruefully. "You heard her." He looked around at the old cabinets and seemed to sigh faintly. "Can we at least get rid of the scallops and scrolls? Streamline it some?"

She squinted, pretending that she was trying to imagine the kitchen without the quaint stylings. Farmhouse was the goal. But modern farmhouse. Not 1960's farmhouse. "I suppose," she allowed, before pointing at the vegetable bin. "That stays."

Josh took a few more measurements and made more notes. "Presumably the harvest-gold paint goes as well as the avocado-green appliances?"

"The sooner the better," Stefan said. "Justine will tell you what she wants."

"It's your—" The rest of her words stopped in her throat at the look Stefan gave her. "Maybe we can choose together," she suggested.

Josh's gaze looked from her face to Stefan's and then down at his notes. "I'll send you a few websites that'll help you figure it all out," he said, his tone neutral in a way that made Justine suspect he was trying to hide amusement.

"Can you get the interior painted before this weekend?" Stefan asked. "My father's coming to visit and I'd like to get at least some improvement. I'm willing to pay for an extra crew."

"If you're willing to pay, the work can get done," Josh said easily. "He staying with you?"

That thought had never occurred to Justine. The extra bedroom upstairs didn't even have a bed in it. Just a lot of Stefan's boxes that were still sealed up tight.

"He'll stay at Hotel Fortune," Stefan predicted.

"They'll all be here for Sunday dinner, though," Justine said. Even Ashley and Megan had promised to come for a few hours.

"Well," Josh glanced around the kitchen. "I can paint, but the kitchen renovation's going to take some time."

Stefan chuckled. "No kidding."

"What about paint colors? Chosen anything yet? I've got a color deck in the truck."

Both men looked at Justine.

She resolutely kept her mouth shut.

"Just go with him," Stefan said. "You know you want to."

"But it's your—" She clamped her lips together when he raised his eyebrow again. Morgan was struggling to get down and she set him on the floor. He took off like a shot for the chair where his giraffe was sitting and pulled himself up to grab it.

"Kid's going to crawl right out of his diaper at that pace," Josh observed.

"What if I choose pink walls and purple ceilings?" Justine asked Stefan.

"As long as you don't add mirrors on the ceilings," he returned smoothly. "Don't want to raise our son in a place that looks like a bordello."

She scooped up Morgan and looked at Josh. "I might have a few paint chips from the hardware store upstairs in my room," she admitted.

Stefan just smiled. "How'd I know that?"

She ignored him and Josh followed her upstairs. She handed over the paint chips.

"You could have just said you chose gray and white," he commented.

"There are a million variations of both colors. Do you know why Stefan didn't just hire an interior decorator? Seems more his style."

Josh lifted his shoulder. "You'd know him better than I do."

That was just the problem. There were times when she was certain that she didn't know Stefan at all.

She pointed at one of the rectangular cards of paint colors. "That gray one is the bathroom and um—" She'd nearly told him *my* bedroom, but suddenly realized that if people really were speculating about her and Stefan, she was providing Josh with a whole lot of information regarding what went on—or didn't go on—underneath their roof. She didn't think of him as a gossip, but people still talked. The conversations at Adam's house were a perfect example.

"All the bedrooms," she said instead. If Stefan didn't like the muted, soft gray tone then she'd repaint his walls, herself.

It was probably the only time she'd have a reason to be in his bedroom.

"And this?" Josh flicked the other cards she'd starred.

"This white for the trim throughout." She tapped the third color—warmer, beiger. "Hallway walls, staircase, the downstairs rooms. Haven't decided about the kitchen but that doesn't matter, not just yet anyway. And if there's anything you can do about getting the paint off the transom windows upstairs, I'd be really thrilled."

He made another note on his pad and pocketed the cards as he headed back to the staircase. "Don't worry about covering furniture or anything. Just clear off breakables and the painters will take care of the rest."

She pulled her hair out of Morgan's fist and followed. "You can really get it all done so quickly?"

His work boots sounded loud in the echo chamber that the staircase was. "If I know my crew—and I do—they'll be out of here Wednesday afternoon. Might want to plan on spending a good portion of the day outside the house."

"We can do that," Stefan said. He was standing at the base of the stairs, eating a plum.

Somehow *he* managed to do it without squirting juice all down his shirt.

Justine walked Josh out to the front porch. Stefan had the brewery and winery matters to deal with. He was always gone for much of the day. If she and Morgan had to be absent from the house for a while, she knew where they'd be spending their time. "Tell Kirby I'll be seeing her at the coffee shop on Wednesday."

Josh gave her a thumbs-up and hopped in his truck.

She went back inside the house.

"Get Morgan into some clothes," Stefan said. "I have something to show you."

She eyed him suspiciously but went upstairs. Morgan really needed a bath, but it could wait until later. She cleaned him up with a damp washcloth that she then used on herself, and in five minutes, she was back downstairs. Fresh ponytail. Sweat-free face. Sweat-free peasant blouse and Bermuda shorts.

He plucked Morgan from her arms and carried him to the truck, before fastening him into his car seat. She realized immediately that they were aiming to the site of the brewery and felt her jaw drop when he stopped his truck a short while later.

"It looks huge!"

Construction crews were busy but what had been just a bunch of pipes in the ground at the beginning of the month was now a skeleton of an actual building. They got out of the truck and Stefan handed Morgan to her.

His grin was as wide as Morgan's had been over the plum tree birds. He held out his hand. "Want to go through it?"

When he smiled like that, she was afraid she would go with him pretty much anywhere.

Before she could place her hand in his, though, Morgan leaned forward, his arms extended. He squealed a bunch of nonsensical sounds.

Stefan was clearly startled. "Does he want me to hold him?"

Justine couldn't be bothered to hide the moisture

collecting in her eyes as she laughed. "Think he's giving you a resounding yes."

Stefan squinted a little, and lifted Morgan out of her arms.

The baby grinned and smacked his hand against Stefan's chin.

When it came to Morgan and strangers, Esteban Mendoza was obviously exempt.

Morgan took one look at his grinning silver-haired grandfather when he arrived at their newly painted house the following weekend and went immediately into his arms.

Stefan met Justine's eyes. "My father," he said dryly. "Always showing off."

Justine didn't know about that. But over the course of the evening, it was hard not to be charmed by the man.

He had them all laughing as he regaled them with details from his trip to Costa Rica and having to talk his way out of a punch in the nose from his traveling companion's jealous suitor when they returned.

"You neglected to mention the punch in the nose before," Stefan said as he refilled wineglasses.

They didn't own a table yet, and certainly not one large enough to seat everyone, but Stefan had borrowed a round table from the Roja banquet room that they set up on the front porch where the setting sun wouldn't be in their eyes.

Esteban waved his wineglass. He'd drunk surprisingly little, Justine noted. "Some things, you know, a father doesn't tell his sons."

"No, you just tell his sons' women," Stefan countered and Justine had to pretend that butterflies weren't swooping all around inside her as everyone laughed.

She'd worried that the simple menu she'd planned of salad and homemade lasagna would be *too* simple. But the pan sitting in the middle of the big round table was decimated and Ashley joked that she wanted Justine's recipe to pass along to their head chef at Provisions.

Megan helped her bring out coffee and the dessert, which was an equal success. The dessert was, anyway. Justine had warmed the blackberry-plum tart slightly and served it with vanilla ice cream that she'd bought special at the ice-cream shop down from Kirby's Perks.

The coffee?

Not so much.

She should have gotten that from Kirby's Perks, too.

"We need to teach you about café Cubano," Esteban said with a wink. "Much better than anything that comes out of a coffee maker."

Justine immediately thought of the restaurant in Little Havana. She could tell that Stefan was thinking of it, too.

Was he thinking about what had followed?

She certainly was.

Constantly.

Even though Josh Fortune and his crew had finished painting the entire interior of the house—even the kitchen despite it being slated for remodeling in the near future—Stefan only showed off the downstairs rooms to his family. She couldn't help but think that he, too, wanted to avoid advertising their sleeping situation.

She put Morgan down to bed and headed back downstairs, listening to the laughter and easy way they had with one another.

The Mendozas were all close. Loving. In each other's business sometimes, but in comparison to her own somewhat distant relationship with her own brothers?

Night and day.

She went out onto the porch and took her seat again beside Stefan. He was debating some point with his dad, and she doubted he was even aware of the hand he stretched across the back of her chair, or of his fingers threading lightly through her hair.

But she was.

Ashley and Rodrigo were the first to leave, but that soon set off the exodus of the others.

Justine stood with Stefan on the porch steps next to the profusion of sweet-smelling flowers and waved until they were out of sight. "Why doesn't your father stay with you?"

He smiled wryly. "No ladies to chat up at the bar."

He helped her carry everything inside and even

offered to load the dishwasher. It might be ugly and green but it still worked. "Thanks for all the work you did."

"I enjoyed it," she admitted. Those butterflies were back in her stomach again. "You have a very nice family. I—I'm glad Morgan is a part of it."

His green gaze slid her way as he leaned over to place a glass in the dishwasher. "You're a part of it, too, Justine."

Butterflies became birds with serious wingspan. "Not technically."

He straightened and she waited, painfully breathless, for him to remind her that she'd been the one to refuse his proposal.

But that had been nearly a month ago now.

But he said nothing, and she swallowed the knot in her throat. "If you're sure you've got the dishes covered, I'll just, uh, just go up now," she said.

He nodded, still focused on his task. "I have meetings starting early but I should be home before Morgan's afternoon nap. Maybe we can grab lunch with Dad at Roja."

She bobbed her head. "Sure." Just that one word felt difficult. Following it up with a garbled "G'night," was even more so.

She was so used to knowing which floorboards to avoid now, that she was able to creep into Morgan's bedroom without making a single sound.

He was sprawled on his back, hands above his head, hair tumbled over his forehead. She lightly tugged down his T-shirt and kissed him one more time before pulling the door nearly closed and going to her own room. The smell of fresh paint was barely noticeable, and she stood at the darkened window for a long while, looking out at the starry night. She was much too restless to sleep.

She had no assignments due until her next online class started in a few weeks and she was entirely caught up with her tasks for her clients.

She blindly grabbed a clean nightshirt and her knee-length sweater and crossed the hallway to start a bath. But even after soaking in bubbles until her fingertips got pruny, she still felt on edge.

She returned to her bedroom and was pondering what boring documentary to stream on her phone that would help put her to sleep when she heard a soft creak outside her bedroom door.

Her breath stopped up in her chest and she stared at the paint-free transom window. There was nothing to see through it but she could practically *feel* Stefan standing on the other side of the door.

But after a moment, another creak sounded as he moved away from it.

She didn't know what possessed her, but she yanked open her door and stepped out into the hall.

There was only the too-dim light from the stairwell to see by, but it was enough.

Stefan turned and looked at her. "I thought you were asleep."

"No." She suddenly wished that she had a pretty

nightgown. Something more feminine than an over-size T-shirt that—she flushed all the way down to her toes with realization—belonged to him.

He took a few steps back toward her. "I just wanted to give you this." He held out a small box.

Smaller than a bread box.

Much larger than a ring box.

"What is it?"

"Just something I—" He exhaled and extended it a few inches more. "Open it."

She took the box and lifted off the lid and felt something inside her squeeze hard. She removed the bracelet from its nest of softly shredded tissue. She didn't need more than the shadowy light to recognize it and was glad of that same light for hiding the way her hands shook as she slipped the bracelet over her wrist.

The blue moonstone seemed to glow.

She looked at him. "Why?"

"You liked it."

She swallowed hard again. Then closed the distance between them. "Thank you," she whispered and reached up to kiss his cheek.

Her lips tingled. He needed a shave.

She went back down from her tiptoes.

"Jus—"

Then she didn't know who moved first. But his mouth was on hers and the newly painted wall was at her back as he pressed against her and the relief of his touch, his taste, was so great she could have wept.

"Tell me to stop," he muttered, dragging his hands up her thighs. Her hips. Up, up beneath the soft T-shirt where she was entirely bare.

"I can't," she breathed and pulled his mouth back to hers. "I can't."

His fingers grazed over her breasts. Her nipples. Then his mouth followed, sending her need careening toward the edge. For months—more than a year—she'd dreamed about him. Even when she'd been certain their paths would never cross again.

She pushed his shirt off his shoulders and found his belt and it jangled softly as she yanked it free. Somehow she managed his fly. "You didn't wear jeans in Miami," she muttered inanely, but he seemed to understand and laughed softly as he kicked them aside. And then his hand was between her thighs, finding her wet and wanting and so, so needy that she couldn't contain a soft cry.

He kissed her again and lifted her right off her feet as he pressed her against the wall. Filled her as easily, as certainly, as divinely perfectly as he'd done all those months ago.

Tears slid from the corners of her eyes and the wood floor creaked softly beneath his feet as he slowly moved inside her until she splintered apart in his arms.

Only then did he let himself go, his mouth on her shoulder. Her neck. And he whispered her name like it was a prayer. "Justine."

Chapter Thirteen

After, he carried her back to her bed and peeled away her T-shirt as if he were unwrapping a gift.

"I've thought about you so many times," he said.

Her throat was too tight for words. She wrapped her fingers around his wrist and pulled him down beside her. She couldn't regret what had happened in Florida.

She wouldn't regret what was happening now.

Already, she could feel him hard and insistent against her, but he was in no hurry.

He threaded his fingers through her hair, stroking it tenderly away from her face. He kissed her forehead. Her temple. Her cheek. Sweet. Light. Gentle. Until tears slid silently from the corners of her eyes.

"Stefan. Please."

"Tell me you thought about me, too," he murmured.

She pushed his shoulders and they slowly rolled. Until she was draped over him. Her breath was uneven as she reached between them. "I thought about you," she whispered and guided him to her. "I never stopped thinking about you."

He inhaled sharply and tightened his hold.

The first time was all rush and sensation.

Now, the second time, was no less sensation. But long. Achingly slow. And when they shattered together, she was afraid she would never be the same again.

Never had Stefan wished more that he could blow off a business meeting than he did the next morning.

But he had other people counting on him to do his job, so he forced himself out of Justine's bed.

He silently returned to his room, gathering up the clothes still lying in the hallway. He showered and shaved and dressed and went into Morgan's room like he did every morning, but his mind never stopped thinking about her.

Through meetings with the Grayson Gear folks and then the construction foreman and Adam at the brewery, he never stopped thinking about her.

Before, Justine had been the fantasy that always hovered in the back of his mind.

Now she was front and center. A live, breathing part of his life. She was in his house. He was in her bed.

It was everything he'd been waiting for.

He rescheduled his last meeting and headed home.

When he got there, she was barefoot in his kitchen, but hunched over the counter, shoulder to shoulder with another man.

He cleared his throat and his father and Justine looked over at him.

Her caramel eyes seemed to glow from inside as they met his and he felt the impact somewhere in the middle of his chest.

"Esteban's teaching me how to make proper Cuban coffee." She stepped aside enough for him to see the electric moka pot they'd been hovering over. "This is the third batch," she admitted.

Stefan nearly choked. Maybe it was his solar plexus that still felt punched. Maybe it was the shock of thinking she'd keel over from caffeine overdose any second. "That you've *drunk*?"

She waved her hand as if he was being ridiculous. "Of course not."

"The first two tries were just fine," Esteban said with a shrug. "But she said they weren't quite like the one she'd had with you at Morgan's so...down the drain they went." His smile was sharp. "Never smart to get in the way of what a woman wants."

Stefan breathed a little easier, but not that much easier. God only knew what tales Esteban might've been telling her. "Never smart," he agreed, yanking his tie loose. It was feeling particularly constricting.

Meanwhile, Justine had turned her attention back to intently watching the moka pot. She'd opened the lid, so it must be getting ready to push out the first droplets of steaming brew.

The pot didn't look new. Neither did the silver cup she was slowly twirling between her fingers as she studied her project.

He wondered where his dad had come up with them. Neither one of the pots his dad owned—both in Miami and at the apartment he kept in Austin—was electric.

He realized he was watching Justine's hips sway slightly back and forth in time to the soft music coming from somewhere.

Salsa.

God help him.

"Morgan sleeping?"

She shook her head and pointed toward the family room. "Your dad brought it. Morgan *loves* it."

It was a portable play yard with mesh sides. And it currently had a three-inch deep layer of plastic balls in it that Morgan was crawling over and tossing around and trying—extremely unsuccessfully—to bite into.

"We'll see how much we love it when he throws those balls all over the place."

Justine laughed. She was back to watching the moka pot again, her curvy hips swaying once more.

He was going to have a heart attack before he reached the ripe old age of thirty-one.

Ignoring the knowing look in his dad's eyes, he muttered something about nothing and left the room.

He ended up in the office.

Justine's laptop sat open on her side of the desk. A pint-size milk bottle held a few sprigs of blue flowers that he recognized from the ones she'd been growing in the garden.

She'd filled half of the shelves on the wall unit he'd ordered. He knew she'd left the other half to him, but all of his crap was still packed away in boxes.

He knew if he said the word, she'd take care of those, too.

That was just Justine. His Justine.

Giving. Kind. Loving.

Especially loving.

He grabbed one of the boxes and tipped it out onto his side of the desk.

Along with old cell phones that he couldn't figure out why he'd kept and files from the accounts he managed and two golf balls, the bridal magazine fell out. Almost like it was a divine message.

If it wasn't for the ads he placed occasionally for Mendoza Winery, he would've never cracked the cover of a bride's magazine. Why the hell would he have wanted to?

He tore off the wrapper and flipped a few pages.

Fancy dresses. Simple dresses. An alarming number of really stupid-looking dresses. There were brides with bird feathers in their hair. Brides with sequins glued to their eyelids.

He closed the magazine again and shoved it, along with everything else he'd just dumped out, right back into the cardboard box.

The truth was, he didn't need a magazine to imagine Justine wearing a wedding dress.

He didn't need a magazine to imagine anything.

"Stefan, you going to try this or not," he heard his dad yell.

He returned to the kitchen where Justine was vigorously stirring the mixture of sugar and coffee inside the small silver cup. Her tongue was tucked between her teeth as she concentrated.

"That's it," Esteban said, nodding his approval. "Little more now. See how it's getting thick and—"

"—peanut butter goopy," she muttered, stirring even more vigorously. She was putting her entire body into it.

"Okay now." Esteban's head was nearly touching hers as they both peered into the little cup. "Let's add the rest of the coffee—slowly. Stir just a little. Little more. And—" He raised his head and held up his hands in a silent hurrah as he muttered reverently.

Even before his father beckoned him closer and Justine, beaming ear to ear, handed him the first taste of the heady, unbelievably exquisite results, Stefan knew what he was going to do.

And how he was going to do it.

* * *

In the end, it took him a few more days than he'd planned. But that was only because the skies suddenly opened and it rained for two days straight.

But by Friday afternoon, the weather was clear again and the garden hardly needed any help to look perfect at all.

"I don't know about this," Mark murmured as he helped Stefan fix a garland of white roses around the iron gate. "I know you're the last Mendoza to marry but are you *sure* this is the right way to go about it?"

"Doesn't matter if I'm the first, middle or the last." Stefan knew how to sell a plan and this was his biggest one ever. He directed Rodrigo who was carrying a huge bouquet. "Set them around the base of the plum tree."

He'd ordered four of the bouquets. Yeah, they were larger than he'd thought they'd be, and more formal, too, but they would still do the job.

So would the one that he'd stuck in the refrigerator that Justine would carry. He'd had to clear out the entire top shelf to fit the thing in there.

"When're the girls getting back?" he asked for about the tenth time.

It wasn't every day a guy planned a surprise wedding. It was fair to be wound up more than usual.

"Ashley says they'll be here by four," Rodrigo said, leaving to get another one of the bouquets from the porch where the florist had unloaded everything a short time ago.

Less than an hour to go.

Ashley and Megan had agreed to keep Justine busy with a spa day at Live and Let Dye. Laurel had agreed to babysit Morgan. She'd promised to be there before four.

Everything was running like clockwork.

He glanced at his phone. He'd never relied too much on lists, but he'd gained a new appreciation for them since he'd started this particular course. String quartet would be in place by three-thirty. The dress had already been delivered by a boutique from Austin—for an exorbitant fee, of course, but he hadn't minded.

He glanced over at Esteban who was sitting on the new garden bench that had replaced the disintegrating one. He was reading a racing magazine and shaking his head periodically. It wasn't clear whether it was the articles or Stefan's plan that had him muttering dire predictions under his breath.

"How're you dealing with the marriage license?" Mark was finally finished tying the bows around the garland to keep it in place.

"County clerk agreed to issue it here."

"Thought there was a waiting period."

"There is." Stefan adjusted his cuff links. His suit coat was still inside. He'd put it on when Justine put on her dress. "The officiant I hired agreed to do the pretty stuff today and the legal stuff Monday afternoon at the courthouse. He'll be here by four. Says it's not a problem."

Mark still looked skeptical. "I get the whole wannabe romantic thing you've got going here, Stef, but what happens if she doesn't—"

"She won't," Stefan said. He was certain.

Justine loved him. She'd have never made love with him again otherwise. Since the night he'd given her the bracelet, they hadn't slept apart once.

"I'm going to watch for the musicians." He went out to the front of the house and paced. The time had been flying earlier, but now it crawled. He fingered the wedding rings in his pocket. He'd guessed her ring size, same as he'd guessed her dress size. But he had a good eye for that sort of thing in general and Justine in particular.

The quartet finally arrived, and they set up near the garden and began playing.

Laurel and Adam got there next, looking a little harried, with ten minutes to spare. She handed over Morgan who was not dressed in the small suit to match Stefan's that he'd planned.

"He cried whenever I tried to put it on him," Laurel said, looking apologetic. It was on a small hanger and she handed it back to him. "Maybe you should try," she said before hurrying around the house after Adam and Larkin.

Stefan wanted the guests in place before Justine arrived.

Ashley sent a text that they were on their way.

Five minutes out.

He took Morgan inside. "We both need a hair-cut, bud," he muttered, as he checked their appear-ances in the mirror. He knew from his own hair that brushing the boy's curls would only make them look more uncontrolled.

What the hell. He pulled off his tie and freed the button at his neck. If his son was wearing shorts and a T-shirt, his son's father could get by without a coat and tie.

Morgan obviously approved, patting Stefan's cheeks with both hands and offering a wet kiss.

He retrieved the big bouquet from the fridge just in time to notice a car pulling up in front.

He hustled out to the garden and exhaled.

His dad had put away the racing magazine and was standing near the plum tree where he'd been assigned. A middle-aged man in a suit stood next to him.

Stefan hadn't realized the officiant had arrived.

Someone had spread the rose petals around on the ground, making a path toward the garden gate.

He was sweating a little even though the after-noon wasn't excessively hot.

Then he saw Ashley and Megan coming around the house. Justine was laughing at something they were saying. She was wearing denim shorts and a blouse with puffy sleeves, and he could see the moonstone bracelet on her wrist.

The rings felt like they were burning a hole in his pocket.

Then she turned toward him, laughter on her face, sunshine in her hair.

And froze.

He walked toward her. Morgan in one arm. Bouquet in his other hand.

Her gaze flicked past him. "What is this?"

It was perfectly obvious. "Our wedding."

Ashley and Megan scurried past them, faces averted as if they didn't want to intrude on the moment.

Justine shook her head slightly. "Our...wedding," she repeated carefully.

"I handled everything," he said. "Your dress is in your room. Ecru lace. That's what the designer calls it." Stefan had just seen a picture of it on the designer's website and had known it belonged on Justine when she became his wife. "I know it's perfect, but just in case, there's a backup hanging in the spare room."

Justine's eyebrows rose slightly. "How...thoughtful."

He'd covered all the angles. "All you have to do is go up and change." He tugged at his collar, glad he'd ditched the tie. "Or stay as you are." She was perfect, wedding dress or not.

She looked past him again and closed her eyes as if she couldn't believe it.

Then she lifted the bouquet out of his hand, turned on her heel and strode away.

He exhaled. Smiled at Morgan and patted their palms together. "Hi five, buddy."

Morgan's lip pushed out. Huge tears hung on his lashes.

Stefan jiggled him. "Come on, Morgan. No tears, okay?"

His son opened his mouth and let out an ear-piercing wail.

He looked at his dad. Esteban was his best man. "Just gonna be a few more minutes," he said.

Esteban waved a magnanimous hand. "Whatever you think, son."

Morgan was doing everything he could to wriggle out of Stefan's arms as he screamed bloody murder. Couldn't even hear the string players.

Stefan carried him inside and shut the door.

Justine was standing in the kitchen. No wedding dress. Nothing but a bouquet that was upended in the sink and color that flagged her cheeks.

Morgan was trying to launch himself toward her and she stepped forward and took him, then backed away as if she needed to protect him from Stefan. "I *never* agreed to marry you!"

"Yeah, but that all changed," he said. He pointed to the ceiling. "Pretty much directly above this spot."

Her gaze flickered. "So *that's* what it was all about? Use a little—" her teeth bared for a moment "—or a lot—of sex to get Justine to say yes to the dress?"

"I'd prefer you say *yes* to me." He couldn't keep the edge out of his own voice. "I told you from the get-go that we should get married."

She was swaying back and forth trying to soothe Morgan, but he wasn't having it. "And I told you from the get-go that I would never want a marriage of *convenience*!"

"Not feeling very convenient now," he said through his teeth.

"What else do you need, Stefan? I gave you unfettered access to Morgan. Signed the paperwork for your paternity. For joint custody. What's the *point* of that charade out there?" She gestured wildly toward the windows that he was glad as hell were closed or everyone outside would have heard her yelling. Her golden-brown eyes glittered with tears. "Well?"

He threw up his hands. "What do you want from me, Justine?"

Her lips parted. Her throat worked.

"If you don't—" She shook her head and sniffed. "Nothing," she muttered. "Nothing at all."

Then she snatched up her backpack and Stefan's alarm nearly shot off the top of his head. "Where're you going?"

"Anywhere." She spun on her heel and walked out of the kitchen. "Anywhere that's away from you!" A moment later the front door slammed so hard the walls shook.

He went into the parlor. Saw through the front window as she opened her back car door and fastened Morgan into the car seat. She didn't look at the house once as she threw the backpack into the front, climbed in after it and drove away, dust billowing behind her.

She'd come to her senses. Cool down. Realize that she'd overreacted.

"She'll be back," he muttered.

She had to be.

Kirby, Annette and Rebecca stared at Justine as if they couldn't believe what they were hearing.

"Stefan surprised you with a *wedding*?" Kirby looked out the window of her coffee shop for a moment. "Would that even be legal?"

Justine folded her arms on the table and dropped her head onto them. "Probably not," she mumbled. Everything that she'd warned herself against was marching through her head and the drum major was screaming *don't fall in love!*

She lifted her head and propped her cheek in her hands. Morgan was playing with the building blocks in the corner with Violet. He didn't know his mama's world was shattering.

"Who all was there?" Annette couldn't seem to stop her morbid fascination any more than Justine could stop herself from recounting the details.

"Rodrigo and Mark for sure, because obviously, Stefan managed to con Ashley and Megan into keeping me occupied." She stared at her glittery pink nail polish. It looked ridiculous now but for some reason she'd let Lindy talk her into it. "Esteban, no doubt. Laurel was babysitting Morgan, so her and Adam.

I think that was it." She closed her eyes, envisioning the quartet of string players off to one side of the garden that seemed to be exploding with formal white roses. "I don't even like roses," she muttered. "The smell gives me a headache."

"Does he know that?" Rebecca asked.

Justine spread her fingers in a helpless sort of answer. "If he really wanted to marry me, wouldn't he think I might want *my* friends and family there, too?" She rubbed her eyes, knowing she was smearing the mascara that Lindy had brushed on so expertly, but not really caring. "I mean, I really like his family and Adam and Laurel, but—" She broke off again and blew her nose on a napkin. "I didn't know where else to go," she said.

Kirby squeezed her hands. "What're friends for?"

Justine laughed brokenly. "Who knew it was to escape the attack-wedding?"

"It wasn't really an attack though," Rebecca pointed out, ever reasonable.

"I won't marry someone who doesn't love me!"

"Maybe he does," Annette said. "He tried giving you a *wedding*. What kind of guy does that? Right down to a wedding dress?"

It had been beautiful. She'd raced upstairs to see if he'd really done something so…so…she didn't have a word for it.

But there it had been. Spread out on the foot of her bed. Simple. A little old-fashioned. She'd seen the small tag sewn into it. It didn't look like something he'd bought off a rack or ordered from the webbernet.

She hadn't bothered to look at the backup dress in the spare room.

She let out another groan and swiped her cheeks again. "I'm going to have to go back. All of Morgan's stuff is there. My things. How can I even face him?"

"Face who?" a gruff, familiar voice asked, and they all turned to see Martin entering the coffee shop. "Y'all look like you're waiting for a funeral. Guess it won't be mine just yet."

Kirby had popped out of her seat and quickly provided him a chair. He sank onto it, wheezing a little, and squinted at Justine. None of them really noticed Kirby turning the sign to Closed and locking the door.

"So?" Martin asked. "What's got you looking so miserable, girl?"

Justine shook her head. "I can't even."

Annette shared the woeful tale. What she knew of it.

"I tell you how you face him," Martin said with surprising force. "You get back in there and tell him you don't settle for less'n you deserve. You don't have t' marry anyone. Not for security. Not for nothing."

She reached over and squeezed his hand. "If it was only that easy. I have to consider my son, Martin."

He scratched his grizzled beard. "What's hard?"

"You can't make someone fall in love with you just because you wish it," Kirby murmured.

His lips twisted and he fell silent.

"I'm going to have to go back," Justine said again.

"Perhaps give it a little while," Rebecca advised. "A cooling off, if you will."

Justine exhaled. "I guess I could go to the Hotel Fortune for the night." Stefan's first child support payment was in the bank. She'd promptly invested it in an account for Morgan's college fund, but that still left her with her own earnings. *One* night in a hotel wasn't going to wipe her out.

She pinched her burning eyes. She hadn't forgotten the high rents in *Rosie Rentals*. She'd call her brothers for help if she had to. Her mother would be a last resort.

"Or you could stay with me," Martin suggested gruffly.

She dropped her hand and stared at him. "Martin, that's too generous. I couldn't impose like that."

He harrumphed. "I got room. Not like what you're used to, probably, but enough for you and the little tyke. And it's not imposing if I invite you." His expression tightened. "Fact is, the doctors don't want me living alone these days. Say they're worried I'm not capable."

She didn't think her heart could hurt any more than it did. "Then I accept," she said softly.

They all gave her relieved looks. She wasn't sure if they were more for her sake or for Martin's.

Chapter Fourteen

She stayed away from Stefan for three days.

In one way, the longest three days of her life.

In another, the most comforting days she'd had in a long while.

Martin, sweet man that he was, did his best to entertain her with stories from his youth. And one afternoon while she was fixing his lunch, she even caught him holding Morgan's hands, encouraging him to walk. It hadn't lasted long; Morgan wasn't that steady yet. He had more speed on his knees.

In the evening, after Morgan was down for the night, sleeping in the portable crib she'd borrowed from Kirby's storage closet, they'd pored over Martin's collection of postcards that he'd collected from all over the world. "I had no idea you'd traveled so much, Martin. Were you ever in love? Did you ever marry?"

"Love and marriage." His gaze had turned inward. "Don't always go hand in hand. Ought to." He shook his head and handed her a small stack of postcards from the early 1900s. "You can have those," he said before turning in for the night.

She'd fanned them out on the table but she hadn't really been seeing them.

Love and marriage.

So often *not* hand in hand.

On the fourth day, after Martin had eaten lunch and he was snoring softly in his favorite chair, she and Morgan drove back to Stefan's.

It was the Fourth of July. The whole town was celebrating the Independence Day holiday with a day-long festival. Mendoza Winery was a sponsor.

Borrowing a few outfits and a crib from Kirby could only last so long. She could get her own clothes. Get Morgan's own stuff. Load up her car with everything she could carry without worrying about running into Stefan.

And then they'd…well, they'd have to see.

No matter how much it would hurt to have to see him, they *had* to find some way of dealing with one another. If only for Morgan's sake.

Stefan had said it all along.

Whatever they did had to protect their son.

She parked in front of the house. Stared at the flowers growing near the steps.

"Mama," Morgan chanted from his car seat. "Go. Go."

She looked back at him. "That's a new one."

He grinned. His two teeth were getting bigger and she was pretty sure he was starting to work on two more.

She freed him from the car seat and they went inside. She knew the house was empty. She could feel it.

The bouquet she'd jammed in the sink disposal was gone. So was the rose garland when she looked out the back windows. The petals on the ground had all blown away.

Morgan's play yard-ball pit was right where it was supposed to be.

She let him down in it and he immediately started throwing balls everywhere, chortling merrily.

At least he was happy.

She passed the jars of plum jam that she'd made before the wedding that were still lined up on the counter where she'd placed them. She wondered if Stefan had opened even one of them.

She went upstairs.

The beautiful lace dress was still lying on the foot of her bed. She fingered the tag sewn into the back alongside the delicate pearl buttons. Anna Kaz Original.

She'd left her moonstone bracelet on top of the gown.

She pulled out her suitcases and packed them but her gaze kept straying back to the dress.

She left the bedroom and looked in the spare room. The dress there was no less lovely. Pure white. Filmy and floaty. It didn't have a tag sewn into the back.

She sniffed and crossed to Morgan's room. She filled his empty hamper with diapers and wipes and some clothes. An infant-sized black suit and gray tie were hanging on the rod in the closet.

There was no question who'd bought it.

She carried the suitcases and hamper downstairs and put everything in her car and went back inside.

Even though she'd intended to pack and run, she couldn't make herself go through with it. She pulled out her phone. Sent Stefan a text message.

He came in less than an hour later.

Faster than she'd expected. But she was sitting on the slipcovered couch from her apartment that they'd put in the parlor and she saw his truck approaching long before he got there.

She lifted Morgan to sit beside her and they were waiting when Stefan opened the front door, his eyes hooded. Wary. He was wearing jeans and a Mendoza Winery T-shirt.

In just four days, he'd nearly grown a beard. It looked so foreign to her, but his green eyes were the same.

"Are you back to stay?"

Of all the things she'd expected, it wasn't that. She opened her mouth to reply but felt stymied.

His lips compressed and he left the room. She heard his boots on the stairs, then the creak of them overhead. She'd almost given up on him returning when he did.

He'd showered. Changed into cargo shorts and a black T-shirt.

He'd shaved.

He crouched in front of Morgan. Held up his hand and tapped it against Morgan's curled fist. "High-five." Stefan's voice was low and gruff.

Morgan babbled and batted at Stefan's hand.

She looked away, battling tears. How were they going to find their way through this?

"Missed you, buddy," she heard him murmur and felt him sit on the other end of the couch.

Morgan between them.

"I'm sorry for the wedding," Stefan finally said.

"So am I," she said thickly.

"They all gave me a rash of sh—" He sighed. "Pretty sure my father thinks it was a learning experience."

"What'd you learn?"

"Hell if I know. You can lead a bride to the altar but you can't make her say I do?"

She laughed brokenly and swiped her eyes. She'd say those words in a second if he only loved her, too. "I don't like roses. But I liked the dress."

"But you wouldn't wear it."

There was nothing she could say. The truth was in the history books now.

"I appreciate you letting me know where you were staying," he said. His voice was gruff.

She'd informed him through a text message. Speaking to him had been out of the question. She'd needed time.

"Martin's dear," she said. "But he's not the solution." Though she had sent a letter on his behalf to his doctor because, aside from a tendency to mix up his medications, he seemed capable of living on his own. There were ways of solving the medication issue.

"What is the solution, Justine?" He looked at her, his expression raw. "Tell me. 'Cause I don't know what else to do."

"I don't want a pretend marriage," she whispered.

"Then what about a real one?"

Her breath stopped, right along with her heart. She stared at him.

"Just listen." He looked uncommonly uncertain as he clawed his fingers through his hair. "Morgan deserves both of us."

"He deserves everything."

"And I don't want you sleeping in another room."

She chewed her lip. "I don't either," she managed.

"So forget the platonic thing. It wouldn't have worked."

"No."

He stood and paced in front of her. "We can make this work, if we want, Justine."

"Dada!"

Justine looked at Morgan. Stefan looked at Morgan.

Morgan held up his arms.

Justine swallowed and watched Stefan. His eyes glittered as he lifted their son.

"Yeah." He laughed. "That's me. Dada."

All the fight drained out of her in the face of one "dada." Her father hadn't stayed around to hear her say the word. Didn't her son deserve more?

"Okay." She felt faint as she said the word. She dashed her cheeks. "But in a church. With a minister. Proper. This is the best thing for Morgan." She would just have to love Stefan enough for both of them. Because there was no point pretending she didn't love him. "And no roses."

Morgan was kissing Stefan's cheek. "Anything you want," he said.

She smiled but it still hurt.

Everything she wanted was right in front of her.

Strange that it had never felt farther away.

They settled on the third Saturday in July. Just twelve days away.

It gave Justine enough time to handwrite invitations and deliver them to her friends. She called Garland and Debbie. They promised to do their best to get there on such short notice. She debated notifying her brothers and decided not to chance it. If she told them, she'd have to tell her mother, and she wasn't going to worry about whether Kimberly would somehow ruin the only wedding day that Justine planned to have.

She and Morgan continued staying with Martin.

She knew that Stefan wasn't thrilled, but he didn't argue. He'd told her he'd go along with anything she wanted and he was doing his best.

They got their marriage license. Had a meeting with Pastor Beckman at the community church to discuss the ceremony. She tried on the lace dress, expecting it to need some kind of alteration. A loosen here. A shorten there. But it was perfect.

Kirby, who was with her, got misty-eyed. "It was made for you."

Of course it hadn't been, but it was nice to hear, all the same.

And when Justine looked at herself in the mirror while Kirby began undoing the endless tiny pearl buttons that ran down her spine, she *felt* like a bride. With all things possible lying straight ahead.

Maybe it could work. Maybe it would.

The day before the wedding, Martin gave her a wrapped gift and waited anxiously until she'd opened it.

The silver photo frame was heavy. Beautiful. Monogrammed with her initials—JF. But she was about to marry a *Mendoza*...

"You can put your wedding photo in it."

She kissed his cheek. She didn't have the heart to tell him the monogram on it was wrong. She was JM now and she still would be when she married Stefan. She tucked the frame carefully back into the wrapping. She'd find an identical replacement and have it engraved herself. He'd never need to know she'd made the correction.

Garland and Debbie arrived the day before the wedding. They got a suite at the Hotel Fortune and since Morgan was spending the night alone with Stefan— for the first time ever—Justine joined them.

She spent way too many hours glued to her phone screen watching Stefan rock Morgan to sleep after giving him his bottle.

The next day, sitting in front of the hotel room mirror, Debbie did her hair and makeup. "Bit of déjà vu, right?"

Justine stared at herself in the mirror. It was much too easy to imagine all of them in Miami. "Wish Anika was here."

"Don't start," Debbie warned, handing her a tissue. "It took an hour to perfect that nude look."

Garland cleared her throat. "Um… Jus?" She was holding up the wedding dress, checking every last detail.

Justine's stomach sank. "What's wrong?" There was a button missing. A tear. Something.

"Did you ever read the tag?"

"Yes, I read the tag. It's an Anna Kaz Original. She only makes three wedding gowns a year."

Debbie nearly leaped over her massive case of makeup to touch the dress.

Justine spun around in her chair. "*What* is wrong with my dress!"

"Nothing. It's perfect."

She wanted to tear at her hair, but it would ruin the perfectly swept ponytail. Just the right amount of height. Just the right amount of sleek. "Then stop freaking me out!"

"Look." Garland held open the dress, pointedly touching the custom label. "*Annakaz,*" she said, running the name together. Then she sniffed, too and met Justine's eyes. "You still think Anika *isn't* here?"

"Oh, *fudge*," Debbie said, blowing her nose. "Hand me the makeup remover. We're starting over."

The parking lot at the church was nearly full when they arrived.

Stefan had sent a limo to the hotel to pick them up. He hadn't warned her.

"Nice touch," Garland murmured.

Justine had told her best friends to wear whatever they chose. Garland was in a surprisingly sedate— for her—pink sheath. Debbie wore purple.

And Justine wore Anna Kaz.

Laurel was waiting inside the church with their bouquets. "Morgan has had a nap. Two servings of green beans and a full bottle. He's good to go."

"Green beans?"

"I tried the usual orange stuff but he didn't want it."

"It's a day for everything," she murmured, watching Laurel slip through the inner door so she could take her seat.

Pastor Beckman came to check on them. "Are we all ready?" she asked.

Justine adjusted her silver bracelet. Maybe the blue moonstone wasn't exactly the perfect jewelry for the dress, but it was perfect for her because it had been a gift from Stefan. She wore tiny dangling pearl earrings. Antiques she'd borrowed from Emmaline's antique shop. Under her dress she wore the wildly sexy pair of panties that Garland and Debbie had given her.

She had the whole tradition. Old. New. Borrowed. Blue.

She drew in a deep breath. Exhaled slowly. Then nodded at the pastor. "I'm ready."

She gestured for the inner doors to be opened and Justine saw Stefan standing at the end of the aisle while the organ swelled. His gaze caught hers even across the distance and something swelled inside her, too.

They *were* doing the right thing.

She felt the exterior door open behind her with a whoosh and looked back.

All four of her brothers came in.

Her bouquet dropped right out of her hand.

"Good," Lincoln said, dashing his hand over his windblown hair. "Thought we were going to be late."

"What are you *doing* here?"

"Your fiancé called us." Max kissed her cheek. "Looking nice, kid."

"Should'a given us more notice," Cooper said, sliding the knot of his tie up to his collar.

"You always have liked daisies." Damon handed her back the bouquet.

Pastor Beckman leaned in. "Do you need a minute?" she asked in a whisper.

Justine looked back toward Stefan again. Esteban had moved to stand beside him. He was Stefan's best man and he was beaming.

"We're good." Her heart was pounding. But in a good way.

"Got someone to give you away?" Linc asked.

"I do now." She blinked hard. She wasn't going to ruin her makeup. Not after Debbie'd had to redo it already. She took his arm.

Debbie waited until Cooper, Damon and Max entered the church before she held up her bouquet to start down the aisle after the pastor.

Garland gave Justine a quick wink and followed.

Linc squeezed her hand. "You happy, Justine?"

She drew in a shaky breath. "Happier than I thought I would be."

"Probably should warn you that Mom's in there."

She sucked in a breath.

"Front row. Got off the phone with her a few minutes ago. She texted a picture of her holding Morgan. Kid has grown."

Justine hadn't felt truly unsteady until now. She

watched Debbie reach the front of the aisle and give a little double take. No doubt noticing Kimberly Maloney in the house. Garland's reaction was less subtle. Her attention honed in on the front row like a guard dog.

"She feels bad, Justine," Linc said. "She's not going to ruin your day."

The organist suddenly began the wedding processional.

She was glad she had Linc's warning.

She looked at Stefan. His suit was charcoal gray. His eyes looked like the sea. And they were looking straight at her.

She had her family. She had her friends. Even Anika, whose words kept flashing in her mind. And she had Stefan.

"Life's short." She lifted her daisies. "Love hard."

The walk down the aisle didn't take any time at all. One minute she was in the back of the church. The next, Lincoln was handing her over to Stefan while Justine's mom gave her a tearful smile.

She returned it with one of her own and looked up at Stefan. "You can't stop with the surprises, can you?"

"These went over better."

Her heart wanted to explode. "Much." She handed her bouquet to Garland and took Stefan's hand.

The pastor gave them a glance and lifted her Bible. She was a tall woman with a warm voice. Standing two steps above them, she could look right over Stefan's head. "It's my pleasure to welcome all of you today for the union of Stefan and Justine. Marriage is a covenant that should be entered reverently, thoughtfully and—"

"And truthfully," a loud voice suddenly shouted.

Justine jerked. Stefan's expression was as startled as hers as they turned.

Horrified, Justine watched Martin nearly stumble as he walked up the aisle. She started to take a step toward him but Stefan's hand stopped her. He closed his arm around her shoulder protectively.

"You can't get married until you know the truth," Martin said. He seemed to be pushing out the words with all his strength.

Justine met Stefan's eyes. "It's okay. He's confused." She gently pulled away and started toward the old man. "Martin, it's all right. Tell me what's wrong."

His eyes looked red. Agitated. "What's wrong is you've gotta know the truth. I tried to make you see. All of you." He swept his arm out and had to take a steadying step. "But you didn't understand. You don't have to marry anyone. Not just to be sure Morgan's secure. Not just to be sure you are. You got money of your own, girl. More 'n you'll ever need."

She ached inside. "Martin, give me your hand. Let's go sit somewhere. We'll talk."

He shrugged her off. "You didn't pay attention to the *initials*, Justine. JF."

Stefan reached her. He put his hand on Martin's shoulder. "Justine's right, Martin. Let's get you—"

"She's Justine *Fortune*." Martin shrugged off Stefan's grasp. He grabbed her hands, squeezing them hard as he peered into her face. "You and your brothers and your cousin Mariana are heirs to a hidden silver mine in Chatelaine."

"What?" The noise from the guests was growing.

"What's mine is yours; what's yours is mines! I promised your grandpa—my best friend Wendell Fortune—that I'd never tell. But I…*he*…was wrong. All of you need to know. It's the mine, Justine. The silver. It's all there." He leaned over, breathing hard.

"Come on." Justine grabbed him and drew him to the nearest pew where Rebecca and Annette were perched. They quickly slid over to make room for the man to sit. "Can we get some water here?"

"Don't want water." Martin grabbed her hands again. Urgently. "You don't have to marry a man you don't love. Not just to make sure you're secure! You're a Fortune, girl. Don't you get it?"

"Martin, I *do* love Stefan!" She touched his cheek, wanting to make sure that he was hearing her. "I *love* Stefan. He just doesn't love me. Not like that."

Martin leaned back, breathing hard. He pulled on his crooked tie, loosening it. Rebecca and Annette leaned over him, fanning him with their wedding programs.

Justine pressed her shaking hands to her stomach and straightened. Her brothers were lined up like they wanted to do battle. Her mother was trying to hush Morgan who'd started crying, but she looked like she wanted to cry, too.

She turned and looked at Stefan. "Weddings are *not* our thing." She sniffed.

"No, but marriage will be." He held her shoulders. His eyes searched hers. "I've loved you since we first met."

Everything inside her shivered. She shook her head. "No, you didn't. I threw up when we met."

He smiled gently. "I remember. Vividly. I remember everything. *Vividly.*"

"You called me an amateur. You felt sorry for me. That's the only reason you came to my hotel—"

He shook his head. "The only reason I came to you was because I couldn't stay away. But you had plans for your life. You had one use for me." He suddenly lifted his head as if realizing that everyone around them was listening avidly.

His hands slid down her arms to wrap around her hands. He kissed her fingertips. "Five hundred and fourteen days, Justine." His voice was quiet. The look in his eyes naked. Raw. "When I saw you that day in the coffee shop, that's how many days it had been since we were together. Twelve-thousand-plus hours. You were in my heart all the while."

"Morgan—"

"I didn't know Morgan." He pressed their hands to his chest, and she could feel his heart pounding. "Now he's here. But Morgan or no Morgan, you were always there first. Last." He released her hands and cupped her face. Slowly stroked the tears on her cheeks. "More than seven hundred and forty thousand minutes, Justine. It's always been you. I love you. And now we're a family and I'm going to keep loving you for a billion more."

She laughed brokenly. "That's a lot of minutes."

"It's a blink," he whispered hoarsely and pressed his mouth to hers. When he lifted his head again, she realized people were clapping. Catcalling.

"I think that's my brother Damon whistling," she whispered. "He doesn't know how to behave in a church."

His eyebrow twitched and he laughed. "Might be my dad. He's not always proper."

She wiped her cheeks. Makeup was overrated. Waterproof mascara? Worth its weight in gold.

She looked over her shoulder at Martin. "Are you going to be all right?"

He nodded. "Wendell's secret has haunted me too long. Now that you know the truth, I'm gonna be just fine."

Justine looked at their friends. At their families. Her heart was too full to hold it all.

Rodrigo tapped Stefan on the shoulder. "Should've known she'd turn out to be a Fortune," he said. "Soon as you kissed her, that die was cast. Mendozas marry Fortunes."

Laughter twittered through the church.

"Should've known," Stefan murmured. "Will you

marry me, Justine Maloney Fortune? Mother of my son. Keeper of my life. My beautiful Justine."

She reached up and wiped the tears from the corner of his eye. Beautiful Stefan. Keeper of her heart.

She stretched up and kissed him. "Yes."

And suddenly a small, high-pitched squeal filled the church.

"Dada!"

The congregation laughed.

Stefan took Justine's hand and they returned to the front of the church. He took Morgan in his arm and held Justine in his other.

And they said *I do*.

Epilogue

The reception was at Roja.

Everyone attended. Even Martin.

He sat in the back of the room, nursing a water, which was the only thing that Annette and Rebecca would allow him to drink.

They were special girls.

Of course, Rebecca would give him what for if he called them "girls" outright. *We're women*, she'd say with that sort of snooty tone she sometimes got.

He missed spending time with them all at Kirby's Perks.

So what if he hadn't been entirely honest with them in the beginning?

He'd done the right thing now. Mariana. Justine and her brothers. They knew they were Fortunes now.

Just because that name had never brought Wendell any happiness didn't mean it was right for them to live out their lives, ignorant that their grandpa had ever existed.

Better for them to continue thinking he was dead.

A partial truth was better than no truth at all.

At least for now.

He nodded to himself and took another sip of water.

Sometimes it was hard, keeping it all straight in his head. But he didn't want to go to his grave with the weight of that secret still weighing on him.

"Martin."

He looked up when Justine touched his sleeve. Stefan stood beside her, looking protective and not entirely trusting.

That was fair enough, too. And a good thing. There was a time when Martin should've been more protective and less trusting himself.

And more 'n a generation had paid the price.

"You're the prettiest bride I've seen in a long while," he told Justine.

Her cheeks got pink. She set a piece of wedding cake in front of him and sat beside him. Stefan didn't sit. He just kept his hand lightly on her shoulder, like he couldn't stop himself from touching her for a single minute.

"I just wanted to ask you more about what you said at the church."

"That you're a rich young lady?"

Her eyebrows tugged together. She reached up to hold Stefan's hand. "You know me better than that. About Wendell Fortune. Why'd he turn away from his family?"

Martin sighed. "Your grandpa felt like his family name was a curse." He picked up his fork and poked at the cake. "Point is, you know you got history now. Fortune history. Wendell had plenty of descendants."

"Wait. More than Mariana and me and my brothers?"

He focused hard, trying to keep it all straight. "More 'n you. Chatelaine's full of them."

He looked past Justine's surprised expression to see her mama approaching. She was carrying that cute bug of a baby but the look she gave Martin was more than a little tight. Learning that the husband who'd left you alone and struggling with a bunch of kids was worth a fortune probably did that to a woman.

"It's time for your first dance," Kimberly told the couple.

Martin felt a little choked up at the look that Justine gave Stefan.

To have a woman look at a man that way was a gift.

More precious than all the silver mines in the world.

"We'll talk more, Martin," Justine said just before

her husband swept her away and into his arms as *At Last* started playing.

She only had eyes for her man.

That was the way it should be.

Martin took a bite of wedding cake—*delicious!*—and decided he would stick around for a while. He and Justine would talk more. He had a lot of talking to do and not just with her.

Maybe.

Then he looked back at Justine dancing with her new groom. They'd picked up their son and brought him into their embrace.

He smiled, confident now that her love for Stefan was true, and hummed under his breath along with the music. *And here we are in heaven...for you are mine...at last.*

* * * * *

#2917 SUMMER NIGHTS WITH THE MAVERICK
Montana Mavericks: Brothers & Broncos • by Christine Rimmer

Ever since rancher Weston Abernathy rescued waitress Everlee Roberts at Doug's Bar, he can't get her off his mind. But the spirited single mom has no interest in a casual relationship, and Wes isn't seeking commitment. As the temperature rises, Evy feels the heat, too, tempting her to throw her hat in the ring regardless of what it might cost her heart...

#2918 A DOUBLE DOSE OF HAPPINESS
Furever Yours • by Teri Wilson

With three-year-old twins to raise, Ian Parson hires Rachel Gray hoping she'll solve all their problems. And soon the nanny is working wonders with his girls...and Ian. Rachel even has him agreeing to adopt a dog and cat because the twins love them. He's laughing, smiling and falling in love again. But will Ian need a double dose of courage to ask Rachel to stay...as his wife?

#2919 MATCHED BY MASALA
Once Upon a Wedding • by Mona Shroff

One impetuous kiss has turned up the heat on chef Amar Virani's feelings for Divya Shah. He's been in love with her since high school, but a painful tragedy keeps Amar from revealing his true emotions. While they work side by side in her food truck, Divya is tempted to step outside her comfort zone and take a chance on Amar—even if it means risking more than her heart.

#2920 THE RANCHER'S FULL HOUSE
Texas Cowboys & K-9s • by Sasha Summers

Buzz Lafferty's "no kids" policy is to protect his heart. But Jenna Morris sends Buzz's pulse into overdrive. The beautiful teacher is raising her four young siblings... and that's t-r-o-u-b-l-e. If only Jenna's fiery kisses didn't feel so darn right—and her precocious siblings weren't so darn lovable. Maybe it's time for the Morris party of five to become a Lafferty party of six...

#2921 WHAT TO EXPECT WHEN SHE'S EXPECTING
Sutter Creek, Montana • by Laurel Greer

Since childhood, firefighter Graydon Halloran has been secretly in love with Alejandra Brooks Flores. Now, with Aleja working nearby, it's becoming impossible for Gray to hide his feelings. But Aleja's situation is complicated. She's pregnant with IUI twins and she isn't looking for love. Can Gray convince his lifelong crush that he can make her dreams come true?

#2922 RIVALS AT LOVE CREEK
Seven Brides for Seven Brothers • by Michelle Lindo-Rice

When a cheating scandal rocks Shanna Jacobs's school, she's put under the supervision of her ex, Lynx Harrington—who wants the same superintendent job. Maybe their fledgling partnership will make the grade after all?

YOU CAN FIND MORE INFORMATION ON UPCOMING HARLEQUIN TITLES, FREE EXCERPTS AND MORE AT HARLEQUIN.COM.

HSECNM0522

*Stationed in her hometown of Port Serenity, coast guard
captain Skylar Beaumont is determined to tough out
this less-than-ideal assignment until her transfer goes
through. Then she crashes into Dex Wakefield. She
hasn't spoken to her secret high school boyfriend in six
years—not since he broke her heart before graduation.
But when old feelings resurface, will the truth bring
them back together?*

Read on for a sneak peek at
Sweet Home Alaska,
*the first book in USA TODAY bestselling author
Jennifer Snow's Wild Coast series.*

Everything looked exactly the same as the day she'd left.

Though her pulse raced as she approached the marina and the
nondescript coast guard station, her heart swelled with pride at the
sight of the *Starlight* docked there. With its deep V, double chine
hull and all-aluminum construction, the forty-five-foot response
boat was designed for speed and stability in various weather
conditions. Twin diesel engines with waterjet propulsion eliminated
the need for propellers under the boat, making it safer in missions
where they needed to rescue a person overboard. Combined with
its self-righting capability to help with capsizing in rough seas, it
had greater speed and maneuverability than the older vessels. The
boat was the one thing she had total confidence in. And she would
be in charge of it and a crew of five.

The crew was the tougher part. She was determined to gain
their trust and respect. She was eager to show that she was one
of them but also maintain a professional distance. Her father and
grandfather made it look so easy, but she knew this would be her

hardest challenge, to command a crew of familiar faces. People she'd grown up with, people who remembered her as the little girl who'd wear her father's too-big captain hat as she sat in the captain's chair in the pilothouse.

Did that hat finally fit now?

Weaving the rental car along the winding road, and seeing the familiar Wakefield family yacht docked in the marina, her heart pounded. The fifty-footer had always been the most impressive boat in the marina, even now that it was over thirty years old. Its owner, Kurt Wakefield, had lived on the yacht for twenty-five years.

Kurt had died the year before. Skylar peered through the windshield to look at it. Had someone else bought the boat? Large bumpers had been added to the exterior, and pull lines could be seen on deck. She frowned. Had it been turned into some sort of rescue boat?

It wasn't unusual for civilians to aid in searches along the coast when requested, but the yacht was definitely an odd addition. There had never been a Wakefield who had shown interest in civil service to the community…except one.

The man standing on the upper deck now, pulling the lines. Wearing a pair of faded jeans and just a T-shirt, the muscles in his shoulders and back strained as he worked and Skylar's mouth went dry. She slowed the vehicle, unable to look away. Almost as if in slow motion, the man turned and their eyes met. Her breath caught as familiarity registered in his expression.

And unfortunately, the untimely unexpected sight of her ex-boyfriend—Dex Wakefield—had Skylar forgetting to hit the brakes as she reached the edge of the gravel lot next to the dock. Too late, her rental car drove straight off the edge and into the frigid North Pacific Ocean.

Don't miss
Sweet Home Alaska,
available May 2022 wherever
HQN books and ebooks are sold.

HQNBooks.com